55

"What are we doing, Lorenzo?"
She whispered the words.

"I think we're d̶o̶i̶n̶g̶ ̶t̶h̶i̶s̶." H̶e̶ ̶b̶̶ hers until
their lips n̶

A gentle ki̶ this was.
Scarlett tol̶ moment,
denying eve̶ ̶a̶n̶d̶ ̶w̶o̶r̶r̶i̶e̶s̶, all of
their past.

How had this happened to her? How did she yield
to him in her life where she had stood firm, stood
alone very often, and refused, oh, so totally refused
to allow anyone all the way into…her soul? Yet
with this man—who had hurt her and whom she
shouldn't be able to trust at all—Scarlett…let go.

THE BRIDES *of* BELLA ROSA

Romance, rivalry and a family reunited.

For years Lisa Firenzi and Luca Casali's sibling rivalry has disturbed the quiet, sleepy Italian town of Monta Correnti, and their two feuding restaurants have divided the market square.

Now, as the keys to the restaurants are handed down to Lisa's and Luca's children, will history repeat itself? Can the next generation undo its parents' mistakes, reunite the families and ultimately join the two restaurants?

Or are there more secrets to be revealed…?

The doors to the restaurants are open, so take your seats and look out for secrets, scandals and surprises on the menu!

The Brides of Bella Rosa saga continues next month in

America's Star-Crossed Sweethearts by Jackie Braun

JENNIE ADAMS

Passionate Chef, Ice Queen Boss

THE BRIDES
of BELLA ROSA

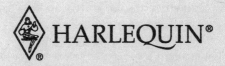

HARLEQUIN®

TORONTO • NEW YORK • LONDON
AMSTERDAM • PARIS • SYDNEY • HAMBURG
STOCKHOLM • ATHENS • TOKYO • MILAN • MADRID
PRAGUE • WARSAW • BUDAPEST • AUCKLAND

Recycling programs
for this product may
not exist in your area.

ISBN-13: 978-0-373-17680-9

PASSIONATE CHEF, ICE QUEEN BOSS

First North American Publication 2010.

Copyright © 2010 by Harlequin Books S.A.

*Special thanks and acknowledgment are given to Jennie Adams
for her contribution to the Brides of Bella Rosa series.*

Australian author **Jennie Adams** grew up in a rambling farmhouse surrounded by books and by people who loved reading them. She decided at a young age to be a writer, but it took many years and a lot of scenic detours before she sat down to pen her first romance novel. Jennie has worked in a number of careers and voluntary positions, including transcription typist and preschool assistant. She is the proud mother of three fabulous adult children and makes her home in a small inland city in New South Wales. In her leisure time Jennie loves long, rambling walks, discovering new music, starting knitting projects that she rarely finishes, chatting with friends, trips to the movies and new dining experiences.

Jennie loves to hear from her readers, and can be contacted via her Web site at www.jennieadams.net.

For the gentle men in my life.
For walking with dignity and grace.
For your strength and integrity and giving.
Most of all for your love. Right back atcha!

CHAPTER ONE

'LORENZO, I sent a message requesting your presence in Luca's office for a meeting ten minutes ago. Did you not receive it?' The words were calm. Professional. They stated the facts and requested an explanation of the man's absence, nothing more or less.

Yes, Scarlett Gibson wanted to tug in frustration on the hot-pink ribbon adorning her ponytail of shoulder-length black hair and, yes, that reaction annoyed her. She hadn't seen Lorenzo for five years. For the next two months she would be working with him. Scarlett had hoped she would be able to do that without caring much about anything to do with him. After all, that was the state she had been forced to reach after he broke her heart five years ago.

Well, Scarlett hadn't become a top financial advisor in Australia by losing her control the first time something annoyed her. But she also hadn't come back to Italy to help out at her uncle Luca's Rosa restaurant, only to have her authority thwarted by the head chef on her first day at the job.

The source of that thwarting stood inside the kitchen of Rosa with his back to her. A slim, muscular back in a fitted black shirt. He wore black trousers, black shoes on his feet. Did he still wear the gold medallion?

Not that Scarlett cared, though she supposed such thoughts were bound to surface. But, surely, they were no different from her wondering if the stranger on the tram beside her back in Melbourne had her coffee made on full milk or skim!

As Scarlett glanced about the kitchen different things began to register. The scents of rich, melted chocolate blended with the warm heartiness of yeasty savoury bread stuffed with tomato and herbs, onion and garlic and olives. Several loaves of the bread were cooling on trays on a bench. Those scents probably explained why Scarlett's tummy suddenly felt a bit odd. She'd have to watch that. She didn't want to eat her way through the next two months. In any case Lorenzo certainly wasn't the reason for her tummy-consciousness.

Three kitchen hands were at work. A woman who looked to be in her thirties, and two men. Scarlett had bumped into the woman inside the restaurant as she appeared to be arriving for work, and had asked her to let Lorenzo know that she wanted to see him in Luca's office without delay.

The woman glanced up now and met her gaze. She didn't look at all guilty or forgetful, which led Scarlett to believe that she had, indeed, passed her message on to Lorenzo.

So what was Lorenzo Nesta's game? Yes, he appeared to be working with great concentration and, yes, there appeared to be quite a bit going on in the kitchen right now. Various desserts in different stages of production littered the bench space around Lorenzo in what appeared to be a very organised kind of chaos.

Scarlett registered this fact, but it was still quite early in the morning. Lunchtime diners were a long way away. Lorenzo should be able to leave his kitchen hands unsupervised at this time of day, with tasks to keep them going, and give Scarlett the time she needed.

Scarlett's sherry-brown eyes narrowed. If Lorenzo thought she would chase after him any time she wanted a few words, he needed a lesson in the order of authority in this restaurant. Scarlett's uncle Luca came first. He was the owner, though he'd told Scarlett that during her time here he didn't intend to come in, just let her get on with what had to be done.

Cousin Isabella had been managing the restaurant a lot of the time anyway. Isabella was gladly taking a step back to focus on her relationship with her newly found reclusive prince, Maximilliano Di Rossi.

Then came Scarlett in the role of business manager.

And *then* came the head chef/assistant manager, Lorenzo Nesta. In other words, where Lorenzo was concerned, Scarlett was the boss!

Scarlett gave a determined nod of her head, only to feel a recalcitrant lock of hair slip loose of its beribboned ponytail.

Confound it all.

Scarlett frowned and blew the lock of hair off her cheek, and glared at that stretch of shoulders in her line of vision.

She had every right to glare. The man was a love rat.

Lorenzo twisted his upper body and glanced over his shoulder at her. 'Just one minute more.'

'Just one more—?' As though she had nothing better to do than stand about and wait for him? Scarlett's brows went up even as she forced her teeth together over the words that wanted to pour out.

Lorenzo held a slender, hollow stainless-steel tube in his hands. He rotated it with long, deft fingers and Scarlett got a view in profile of a manly cheek already darkened with a hint of beard shadow, a strong nose and chiselled lips pursed in concentration, and the downward sweep of thick lashes over eyes that she knew were the deepest, richest shade of brown.

Not that Scarlett had any particular kind of obsession with dark brown. Well, with the possible exception of it swirling around in a mug with a marshmallow melted in the top of it.

'Actually, Lorenzo, I've been waiting ten minutes already.'

Scarlett uttered the words in a calm tone that nevertheless held a hint of steel within it. 'You know the way to Luca's office. I'd appreciate it if you didn't keep me waiting any longer.'

Scarlett wheeled about and made her way back through the kitchen's swing doors, through the rear of the indoor dining area past several potted plants and a nook filled with a warm colourful display of bottles of oils and relishes and sauces, and into the corridor that housed Luca's office.

Mixed feelings walked with her. This return trip to Italy was important to Scarlett for many reasons. She wanted to enjoy Isabella's company and bond with her again and maybe get in a better place with *all of her family here*. If that was even possible after so long? Helping Uncle Luca out felt like a good step towards that. She'd hesitated when Isabella had asked her, and that had been because of Lorenzo. But then Scarlett had decided if she was facing down old demons she could just as easily face down this one at the same time. How hard could it be?

'Scarlett, good morning.' Her cousin Isabella approached as Scarlett put her hand on the office door. 'All set for your first day on the job?'

Scarlett stopped, and regrouped. And smiled, because this was Izzie and they had grown up together. They'd had a lot of girlish fun together before she and Scarlett had done something incredibly silly. The ramifications of which were only now settling. Scarlett had punished herself and had moved to Australia, away from her Italian family and friends to get to know her father and his side of her family.

'Hi, Izzie. Yes, I'm ready for my first day. I didn't expect to see you in here today. You look glowing. How's your prince?'

'Princely as ever.' Isabella blushed a little, but she also smiled and held out her arms. 'I'm rather pleased that I've found him.'

'He's made you happy, so I'm pleased too.' Scarlett stepped into Izzie's hug.

There was an ache in the middle of her chest when she let go.

Coming back here always tugged at her emotions. This time she was here to try to help the family out, with a hope of reconnection hiding some place deep inside her that was perhaps unrealistic.

If it was going to make her feel all mushy whenever she came across a family member, Scarlett had better get that reaction right under control, and fast. 'I have Lorenzo coming in for a meeting. Since you're here, I'd like to speak with you after that, if possible.' Her full lips tightened before she went on. 'I'll probably have questions for you after I've grilled him.'

'Grilled? You won't upset—?' Isabella cut herself off and forced a smile back to her face. 'You're the boss. Of course you should manage things here however you feel is right.' Isabella drew a breath. 'I'm here to put together a batch of Papa's special sauce, so I'll be around for a while. I can speak with you when you're ready.'

'Let's say in about half an hour, then.' Luca's secret recipe sauce was a mainstay of the Rosa restaurant's authentic Italian cuisine. Scarlett wondered what kind of reception she would get when she wanted an accounting of the ingredients list so she could cost-base it.

A *hands-off we're-not-telling* reception, she imagined, from both Luca and Isabella. Well, perhaps they could tell her the costs, but not the ingredients?

'It's nice to have you back in Italy, Scarlett, and I really appreciate all you're going to do for Rosa.' Her cousin's expression tightened. 'The money issues are worrying. Max was prepared to invest a cash injection to get Rosa back in a strong financial position, but of course that would have offended

Papa and it wouldn't have really solved anything in the long term. I couldn't have let Max do that, either, much as I love him for wanting to.'

'Quite right.' Simply throwing money at things wasn't the answer. But with the right changes and improvements, success *could* be grasped. That was what Scarlett believed, and had proved in her own career path as she climbed the ranks to a highly successful financial advisor in Australia, advising some very respectable companies. She wanted the same for Rosa. She wanted the restaurant to run at a profit and be self-sufficient and successful.

Isabella disappeared and Scarlett stepped into Luca's office. It would be her headquarters for the time being, though she didn't intend to be the kind of manager who sat behind her desk all day and didn't watch what was going on around her. Despite her hope to not need much to do with him, she might have to watch Lorenzo Nesta very closely. Particularly if he thought he could get away with stunts like ignoring her summons when she sent it!

'Scarlett—'

And speaking of her nemesis, there he was, standing in the doorway of the office looking a little prickly beneath the surface though she could see he was trying hard to mask that. And, she supposed, somewhat attractive.

Not that he appealed to Scarlett any more in any particular way. He'd killed that reaction in her five years ago. Her heart rate *had* jumped a little just now, but that was as a result of preparing to do battle if necessary.

'Lorenzo.' She gestured to the visitor's chair on the other side of the desk. And really, wasn't she the one to have the right to some prickliness? She'd only just started here, and already he'd put her morning's schedule off centre. 'Please be seated. I want to speak with you about how things have been running here at the restaurant, and how they'll need to be run from now on. But perhaps you'd care to start by explaining why you ignored my request for this meeting.'

'I didn't ignore the request, I just couldn't drop everything and come to you immediately.' His chest expanded beneath the black shirt before he carefully exhaled. Scarlett caught sight of a glint of gold around his neck. *Was it* the chain that he'd had when they first met?

Not that you care, Scarlett.

'Why couldn't you leave your staff for a few minutes?'

'It's not always possible to walk out of a busy restaurant kitchen without consequences.' His words were respectful, but also firm. 'You gave me no notice, just a message that my presence was immediately required.'

'At this early hour of the day I would have thought you'd be able to spare some time.' Scarlett tried to keep her gaze locked on his eyes, yet it wandered to the curve of his lips, the strong nose, the very old, small scar over his left eyebrow and despite her determination, a memory stirred.

He'd held her in his arms one day after they'd made love, and had made up outrageous stories about how he got the scar as a child. Each one had been sillier than the last until Scarlett had needed to hold her sides to try to contain her mirth. The truth was that he'd fallen, not very far or excitingly, off a piece of play equipment at school.

That day, Lorenzo had said something strange to her. *Sometimes the scars you see are better. I'm happy to wear this one. At least it bears no shame.* His gaze had sobered and for a moment Scarlett had felt as though he'd pushed her away, even though she still lay snuggled in his arms. She'd opened her mouth to ask, she hadn't been sure what, but he'd kissed her again and the moment had passed...

Well, that was then, and what was she doing thinking about this now anyway?

Scarlett *wasn't* laughing now. Nor did she want to reminisce about the far distant past of her life. She couldn't afford to be distracted!

'We're very busy in the kitchen today. It's good that Isabella came in. I've asked her to supervise until I can get back.' Lorenzo drew a deep breath. 'At least that's something.'

Did he say that as though Isabella wouldn't know what she was doing in there?

'My cousin has worked in the kitchen of Rosa for a long time.' Isabella could do a just fine job of supervising the staff, or making the meals for that matter. 'Whether she has a whole lot of bits of paper to say so or not, it wouldn't surprise me if she's a more qualified cook than you are.'

Lorenzo made a sound in the back of his throat. 'Of course I trust Isabella in the kitchen. That's not what I meant.'

'Whatever you meant, we're wasting time.' Scarlett glared at him across Luca's desk. If her anger was somewhat of a shield, she wasn't about to admit it.

Lorenzo stared back and whatever thoughts he had disappeared in his eyes. 'By all means, please go on with what you need to say.'

'I will.' Another curl of Scarlett's hair slid from its moorings and lay against her cheek. Scarlett gritted her teeth and asked herself how a few minutes in his company could get her so worked up so easily. She'd just finished telling herself she would treat this in a calm, professional manner.

Lorenzo's gaze clung to her hair for a moment before he raised it to meet her eyes.

Dark brown to sherry brown.

Five years older to aeons wiser.

He'd be thirty-two now. Scarlett was twenty-eight. That extra layer of maturity…flattered him.

'Do you understand the reason for my presence at Rosa?' Scarlett didn't know what Isabella had told him. She doubted Luca would have said much. Her uncle had hidden the state of

Rosa's finances even from Isabella for as long as he could. It had taken effort to get Luca to the point where he was willing to have Scarlett come in to try to clean things up here.

Lorenzo made a 'Who knows?' gesture with his hands. 'You're here as Financial Manager for the time being. Isabella has relinquished her management to you, though she'll still be actively involved in the restaurant in other ways. In other words, you answer only to Luca himself, though he's been quite scarce here of late.'

'Good. You understand, then.' In fact he had a better grip on his knowledge of events than Scarlett had imagined.

Lorenzo examined her face. Maybe he was searching for her response to him? Or maybe he saw a different woman five years on from the one he had known? Well, he'd helped Scarlett to become that woman. Self-contained, determined, career-focused and beyond guarded in some ways. She'd been halfway there before she even met Lorenzo.

'As Head Chef and Assistant Manager you will answer directly to me. Everything you do will be under my scrutiny, and I expect your full co-operation with any changes I decide to make to improve the financial bottom line of the restaurant.' *This* was what needed to be said.

'I run a good kitchen and do my best with the resources Luca has allowed me.' He spoke the words and then clamped his lips together before he added, 'All of us have had to work within the framework of Luca's feelings about employing and buying locally and treating the staff in some ways as a big family.'

And Luca loved to be generous and giving. This was something Isabella had brought up and, though her cousin hadn't gone into much detail, Scarlett had wondered whether this had caused problems for Isabella in her management efforts. Scarlett would look into it.

'I'm accustomed to co-operation, Lorenzo. This morning,

by your actions, you communicated to other members of the staff here that I can wait until it suits you if I request a meeting.' She drew a breath. 'I don't want to have to make changes to the staffing here, but I also will not work with a head chef who doesn't respect my authority.'

Scarlett's message was clear, and clearly received if the tightening of Lorenzo's expressive mouth was any indication.

'We received a special order—' He cut the words off and shook his head. 'My apologies for not attending you immediately. It would be great if in future you could give me a little notice so I can leave the kitchen without any negative impact on the work there, but if you can't, you can't. I will still co-operate with you to the fullest.'

He held her gaze with a level one of his own. 'I value this job. Every step I take is aimed at making the best of Rosa that I possibly can.'

'Then I'm sure we understand each other and will get along just fine.' Scarlett's fingers closed over a typed list on Luca's desk. 'I'd like to discuss the current staffing policies with you. I understand from Isabella that you've been given a fairly free rein to make decisions about the number of kitchen hands employed at any given time, how you roster them, that sort of thing.'

'I have enough kitchen hands to meet the kitchen's needs. Some of them, Luca has speared into the positions when I... might not have chosen them for the work, but I do my best with the workers I have.'

It wasn't a negative statement. Scarlett got the impression it was an honest one.

Lorenzo named staff members. He explained whether they were full or part time, hours they worked and what their roles were. 'There is room for all of them to improve their skills in one way or another. I work on that on a daily basis.'

For a restaurant the size of Rosa, the staffing levels seemed appropriate. 'I'll want to examine your kitchen roster some time in the next day or two.' And the wages and staff conditions, but those weren't Lorenzo's responsibility.

There had to be reasons why Rosa didn't make a better bottom line financially. Scarlett would turn the restaurant inside out to discover those reasons and fix them.

For now she needed to know: 'How economical are you with your cooking methods? What are you doing to reduce ingredient wastage? How often do you have Isabella in to supervise the making of the special tomato sauce?'

'Within the guidelines I have to work with, I believe I'm being quite economical.' Lorenzo stared into Scarlett's sherry-brown eyes and assured himself he could and would finish this interview in a calm relaxed manner no matter how many questions Scarlett threw at him or how less than happy to see him she might appear to be. And no matter how concerned he felt about his job security with Scarlett now in a position to decide his fate.

He didn't need any more ripples in his work record, but what could he do besides work hard and perform to the best of his ability?

Regret tugged at him. It wasn't easy to look into Scarlett's lovely face and keep memories at bay. That was a problem he'd worried over since he first heard she would be coming to Rosa to act as Financial Manager. He wanted to ask how she'd been—was she happy? So many things. He couldn't ask any of those questions. It was all long gone, the mistakes and missteps were made. He couldn't fix the past. And his present.

'I maintain a high standard in my kitchen.' Best to stick to these things with her. Best not to notice her too much, and he was *trying* not to notice how lovely she looked in the prissy cream blouse. She'd teamed it with a deep crimson and cream pinstriped skirt that had clung to her hips as she stalked out of the kitchen minutes ago.

The clothes were businesslike yet still practical for Italy's summer weather. But did Scarlett think the outfit made her look severe? Remote? If so, she didn't have much idea. Her hair slipping from its moorings put paid to that, as did the bright pink ribbon that adorned the silky black mass.

That and the softness that she couldn't quite hide, deep in the backs of her guarded eyes. She might play the tough boss lady, but it was clear she still had…her softer side.

'My reputation and that of the restaurant are on the line with every meal produced.' His tone wanted to soften. He forced it to remain businesslike. His job could be on the line here, which meant he couldn't let himself indulge in memories of the past when, for a time before it all went wrong, he and Scarlett had been happy together.

He forced the words out. 'If a dish is substandard it's thrown away, but my ultimate goal is to ensure everyone on my team works hard enough and carefully enough to always produce a dish worthy of the standards of Rosa.'

'Throwing meals out at all—that'll have to stop.' Scarlett leaned forward in her chair.

'Sometimes things happen even in the best kitchens, Scarlett.' Did she really imagine that could be otherwise?

'Well, I suppose so.' Scarlett's pretty nose scrunched.

'Now and then a patron will throw a fit over a perfectly good meal, too, and send it back.' From time to time, this happened. 'It's important to maintain goodwill, even when we know the restaurant is in the right.'

'Yes, of course.' Scarlett drummed one slender set of fingers on the desk before she stopped the movement abruptly. 'I want to be brought in on it if I'm here and a diner carries on like that.'

So Lorenzo could hide behind her skirts while she took

care of things for him? Pride rose up. He pushed aside all knowledge of the edge of shame that went with it. What did they say?

If you don't acknowledge it, it doesn't exist.

His father was certainly good at that. Well, at ignoring Lorenzo's existence much of the time, now that his son had 'dishonoured the family with his behaviour'. Lorenzo wasn't in a position where he could explain himself to his family.

And now was not the time to dwell on any of that!

'I assure you I am quite able to deal with any difficult patrons here.'

'Well, I know that.' She said it as though any other option was ridiculous.

And Lorenzo realised he might have overreacted. He could thank his past with Marcella for that. Well, he could thank that past for a few things, couldn't he? 'Regarding Isabella making the trademark sauce, I keep her informed of the supply. She tops it up when needed so we make sure we never run out.'

Maybe if he made it clear to Scarlett that he had a good knowledge of the restaurant's workings, she would feel more able to work with him to achieve whatever she needed to here. Lorenzo needed to know just what her goals were and what she would expect of him.

He'd worked closely with Isabella, and she'd handed plenty of responsibility to him. That had suited him, but what did Scarlett want? 'Is the restaurant in real trouble? Are jobs secure? Isabella only said you'd be working to improve our bottom line. She didn't cover the why of it.'

Scarlett hesitated for so long, he'd almost decided she wasn't going to answer. Finally she said, 'The restaurant has been running at a loss, I believe for quite some time.' The moment the words were out, she glared at him. 'You're being trusted with that information because I need your co-operation and full disclosure from you to enable me to do my work here properly and get Rosa back in the black. If you discuss this fact with anyone, or if you hold anything back—'

'What kind of man do you think I am?' Lorenzo's nostrils flared.

But they both knew the answer, didn't they? To Scarlett, Lorenzo was a man who had let her down. The answer shone in her eyes for a moment before she glanced away.

'You won't lose your job due to financial reasons.' Scarlett uttered the words in a low tone. 'Luca and Isabella both speak highly of you and want to keep you here. I am determined to turn the restaurant around so it starts making a profit, and continues to do so. If you prove to be good for Rosa as they are saying you are, and you're respectful to me and my authority, then I'm sure your job will be quite safe, too.'

Her assurance helped somewhat. Scarlett might feel angry towards him because of their shattered past love affair. But if she said his job wasn't in jeopardy provided he continued to work well, Lorenzo *should* be safe. He wished it didn't have to matter so much to him, but it did. He needed every Euro of his wages to help him save for *his* ultimate future. That future was a long way away, years still, but he was doing his best.

So now he only had to make sure Scarlett didn't fire him for any other reason, and he hoped, over time, that she would see his commitment to Rosa.

Scarlett seemed to make an effort to centre her thoughts once again. 'I'm sorry for all the questions, but your answers will help me prioritise how I approach change here.' She drew a breath. 'What are the most popular dishes and how do they stack up in terms of profit margins? Do you buy one hundred per cent only local produce?'

'We always use local produce if possible, otherwise I shop nearby for other things.' The restaurant had a small van for that purpose. He listed the most popular dishes. Many of them used Luca's secret sauce. 'As Luca's rules about local produce have been hard and fast, I haven't looked into how much money we might be losing by buying locally but there are times when I think there would be a substantial difference.'

'I see. Well, thank you. I can see I have a lot of things I need to look into.' Scarlett got to her feet in a single, lithe movement.

Meeting over, apparently. For a moment he wondered if she would shake his hand. But she simply strode to the door in the cream pumps that matched her blouse exactly.

Lorenzo dragged his gaze upwards away from tanned slender legs. 'My history in restaurants has taught me a lot. If you want to discuss any aspect of Rosa at any time—'

'I'll keep that in mind.' Scarlett's brows drew together and she took a half-step towards him before she stopped and tugged the door wider. 'I'll let you get back to work.'

Lorenzo stepped forward too, until he was even with her. The scent of her perfume filled his senses, catapulted him back to happy times between them before the complications of his life had wrecked everything for both of them. Could either one of them hope to truly get through her working here, and just ignore all that? 'Scarlett, the past—'

'Is irrelevant between us now.' She acknowledged its existence and dismissed it with a wave of one hand, all in the space of seconds. 'I can assure you, from my perspective it is long forgotten!'

He might have believed it, he supposed. That Miss Scarlett *Gibson* quite frankly *didn't give a damn*.

Yes, Lorenzo might have believed that if he hadn't seen the burn of hurt deep in the backs of her eyes that had nothing to do with Rosa or now or here, and everything to do with that past.

'I'm glad to hear you're okay with that.' Lorenzo turned on his heel and went back to his kitchen where he at least had the hope of telling himself he was somewhat in charge and in control. He needed that. Marcella's treatment, her behaviour towards him, had left him with the need to…find self-esteem within his work. It was a cliché, he supposed, but Lorenzo was honest enough to admit it about himself.

As for Scarlett's position here as the new boss, Lorenzo wanted to believe the two of them could work together without things turning catastrophic. Surely they could.

Couldn't they?

CHAPTER TWO

'YOU know there'll be fallout for you once Lisa learns that you've moved yourself out of her villa.' Isabella put the middle-sized suitcase of Scarlett's set of three down in the centre of the small bedsit, and turned with raised brows to face her cousin. 'And *I'd* have loved to have—'

'I know. And...thanks. But I would have felt I was intruding.' It was the next morning, early. Max had driven them here, helped them to unload Scarlett's luggage, and had then disappeared with a promise to meet Isabella in the village later.

Or should Scarlett say the prince had driven the princess into town? The romance between his cousin and the reclusive prince *was* a little like a fairy tale. Scarlett stifled a small grin and wondered how she could be so cheerful when a part of her very much did not want to face another day at the restaurant with Lorenzo working under her nose, and making her feel uncomfortable and overly conscious of him by turns.

Not that he'd been trying to do that, to be fair. Being in contact with him had turned out to be more difficult than she had anticipated, that was all. Scarlett dumped her overnight bag and laptop case beside the suitcases. 'It's not up to Mum to decide where I stay while I'm working at Rosa.' Lisa wasn't in Monta Correnti just now anyway. 'Though I do appreciate her inviting me to stay at her villa.'

Isabella raised her eyebrows. 'You mean inviting you in a way you felt powerless to refuse.'

Her accompanying smile reminded Scarlett of girlhood days.

'Maybe Mum did sort of coerce me into agreeing to stay there. But I found a way to get out of being under her scrutiny, even if it was only the second-hand scrutiny of her house staff.' Scarlett had tugged on her ribbon before she thought about it. It was a gold and black polka-dot ribbon today, which she felt nicely offset her black and yellow A-line, knee-length linen dress.

'And anyway, with no offence meant to anyone, I prefer to be here.' Scarlett let her gaze rove over the room. It was small, simply furnished with a sofa that pulled out into a bed, a tiny dining table with two chairs, a kitchenette and a bathroom with a washing machine tucked behind a door at the far end.

Certainly Scarlett's apartment back in Melbourne had been much roomier, and her mother's villa heaps roomier again. Well, she'd sublet her apartment.

And this little bedsit tucked onto the end of a widow's house was clean and neat and serviceable. It would meet Scarlett's requirements for her stay in Italy. Most of all she could be private here at the end of the day. Scarlett wanted to reconnect with her family, but she needed *some* kind of bolt hole! 'I need my own space sometimes, Izzie. Anyway, by the time Mum turns up again I could be halfway through my stay. What she doesn't know...'

'Won't cause an outburst?' Isabella shook her head. 'Have you really forgotten that much of what it's like to be part of a big family with all the related tensions and nosiness and everything else? I know you have your father and his relatives in Australia, but have you also forgotten what Lisa can be like when she unleashes her sharp tongue? Your mamma will hear about you moving out within days, if not sooner.' A hint of annoyance leaked into Isabella's tone.

It wasn't directed at Scarlett, and Scarlett knew this. They were all less than happy with Lisa after the way she'd behaved towards her brother Luca recently.

'I haven't forgotten. Mamma hasn't spoken with my father, even on the phone, since I turned eighteen, but I remember a few of the calls before then. Mum shouting and my father looking as though he'd like to tear his hair out by the end of it.'

Dad had made a good home for her when she decided at twelve that she wanted to go to him in Australia. It had taken time for Scarlett to let herself really love Brad Gibson. She'd been an unhappy, upset child at the time, but they'd got there. Her father was a good man.

Scarlett went on. 'The bedsit is perfect, Izzie.' She gestured about her. 'It's literally less than five minutes' walk from Rosa.' Scarlett walked to the opened door and glanced out. 'In fact, you can see the restaurant from here, if you stand in the part that isn't screened by the overhead lintel and all that flowering creeper. Anyway, shall we go? I need to get to work. I'll unpack tonight.'

Scarlett reached once again for her laptop computer and purse. She perched a pair of sunglasses on her nose. With her eyes shielded from view she felt somewhat better.

'I have an errand to run before I drop by the restaurant.' Isabella gave a soft smile. 'It's just a little something I'm picking up. A photo of me that I had framed.'

'To give to your prince when you meet up later?' Scarlett asked teasingly, and smiled when Isabella blushed.

Isabella smiled, too, and while she was still smiling she said, 'Speaking of photos, Jackie's got heaps of her daughter now. You should—'

'I don't have time to look at photos.' The rejection shot

out of Scarlett's mouth before she even realised how trapped Isabella's suggestion had made her feel. Scarlett found it hard to think about the daughter her sister, Jackie, had given up for adoption.

Because she'd thought, and thought, and *thought* about it over the years and the more she did that, the deeper her guilt seemed to lodge itself. Scarlett had avoided contact with Izzie *and* Jackie for years because of this.

Now they were back in contact, and Scarlett *did* want to be closer.

But a part of her also wanted to demand to know if her cousin truly thought getting over something like that long separation and loss could be so simple for Jackie? So easy? That Scarlett's sister would miraculously have forgotten all the years of feeling as if there'd been a hole left inside her just because now she had her lover back in her life, and some contact with her daughter, Kate? After all, Scarlett and, to a lesser degree, Isabella, had caused Jackie's loss!

Before Scarlett could speak or do otherwise, the sound of a motorcycle echoed through the square.

'I didn't think he'd be in this early.' How stupid, to get all breathless just from the sight of Lorenzo across the square. It must be because he'd made it necessary for her to assert her authority yesterday.

'You recognise him from that distance?' Isabella seemed surprised.

'Who else would it be?' Scarlett dodged having to explain that she and Lorenzo had known each other five years ago, and had *more* than simply known each other. They'd kept the relationship secret and Scarlett wasn't about to reveal anything about it now. 'I mean, he's gone to the restaurant, it's a man and he *is* reasonably recognisable even at this distance.'

'I suppose so.' Isabella followed Scarlett's glance. 'Lorenzo did well yesterday, didn't he?'

Praise for the head chef wasn't quite what Scarlett had been expecting. She said carefully, 'The diners seemed happy enough with their meals.'

'Oh, I'm sure they all would have been.' Isabella waved a hand as though to dismiss this. 'But I meant with that special order for lunch for twelve people. It was *very* last minute, but Lorenzo was sure he could pull it off. I wouldn't have been able to. Not with the things on the menu.'

Oblivious to Scarlett's surprise, Isabella went on. 'The movie star was happy, though. One of the kitchen hands made the delivery and Lorenzo said at the prices he insisted on to do the catering, the restaurant will have cleaned up on it financially.'

A movie star?

A last-minute order for a special lunch for twelve people?

This was the reason why Lorenzo hadn't come immediately to yesterday's meeting?

Why hadn't he said so? Scarlett stared at her cousin as yesterday's impressions realigned themselves. 'I wasn't aware—'

'I thought Lorenzo would have explained it to you. He'd just finished tempering the chocolate rolls when he asked me to take over while he had his meeting with you. I was a nervous wreck even in that short span of time. I can cope with our regular menu, but that?' Isabella's eyes glazed over as she started listing dishes.

'Chocolate tart, limone mousse, a chocolate and hazelnut gateau, vanilla and raspberry chiffon cake, *lime*-custard-stuffed profiteroles, built into a profiterole *tree* if you please, and that was only one course of the menu.' She drew a breath. 'Even with the meeting with you in the middle of it, Lorenzo managed and got flawless results.'

'Oh.' Scarlett found herself in the rare position of feeling as though she hadn't really behaved appropriately in relation to her work, that she'd perhaps brought personal issues into it and allowed those to colour her judgement. That she'd been hard on Lorenzo and hadn't really given him a chance to explain things. That was bad management on her part, and, no matter what her personal feelings might be towards him, he'd shown dedication and commitment to Rosa.

'Well, I'd better get going.' Isabella gave her a quick hug again. 'See you in a while.' She walked off.

'Yes. See you.' Scarlett frowned and started towards the restaurant.

It appears I may have misjudged you yesterday, Lorenzo. Scarlett practised the words in her mind as she pushed open one of the kitchen's swing doors. Lorenzo might have played her false five years ago, and Scarlett wasn't about to forget that. But when Scarlett made a mistake in her work, she admitted it. Now she just had to find Lorenzo, and say those words to his face. Then she could get on with the real work of the day with her thoughts at peace.

It only took a second for Scarlett to realise that her hopes of catching Lorenzo alone were not to be. Two seconds later she comprehended that the conversation being conducted beyond a bank of open shelving was not a happy one.

Lorenzo and another male stood with their backs turned to her. They were unaware of her presence. They spoke in Italian in muted voices that seemed all the more intense for that fact. The young kitchen hand had a backpack dangling from his hand, and Lorenzo plunked two bottles of some kind of spirits down on a work surface before he turned back to the boy.

From the stiffness of Lorenzo's back, and the guilt Scarlett could see written all over the boy even from this distance, it was clear Lorenzo had caught the young man trying to steal the bottles. What was the teenager's name? Scarlett ran her mental list from yesterday's 'meet the staff' moments. Dante…

Scarlett's brows drew together. Was this where Rosa's profits had gone? *Taken by light fingers?* She wanted to wade in, and yet something in Dante's posture and expression, and the way Lorenzo was holding his emotions in, made her hesitate. And the boy was young. He couldn't have worked here all that long. Certainly not long enough to sink Rosa financially through petty theft, even though this *was* a very serious thing to have happen.

As Scarlett stood there Lorenzo's low words carried to her.

'This stunt—' He gestured towards the bottles. 'I can't believe you'd do such a thing. You're not a bad boy, Dante. Not everyone on this team is here by my choice but you're someone I've really wanted to keep. You try hard; you're keen to learn. You've always made your shifts without any problems at all. You'll take direction and you have a natural flair in the kitchen. You have it in you to become a good chef one day.'

'I'm sorry. I know this was stupid. Mamma has this new boyfriend—' The boy cut his words off abruptly and for a moment looked trapped. 'I knew taking the bottles was wrong and I've never done it before. I promise you.' The words were passionate. 'Please, don't fire me.'

'You're the only child at home, if I remember rightly?' Lorenzo said the words as though they meant nothing, yet Scarlett could see enough from the view of his profile to understand that he wanted to know more.

'Yes. I'm an only child.' The boy confirmed this.

'You took Luca's hidden spare key yesterday and came

in to steal the wine this morning.' Lorenzo made the statement flatly. 'Weren't you worried I might catch you? Everyone knows I start earlier than my shifts and often work later, too.'

'I don't know.' Dante shrugged skinny shoulders and then seemed to almost wince as he stopped the movement. 'I guess I didn't think about that.'

But Lorenzo was thinking about that.

And Scarlett thought about that.

Why would this boy, who seemed clever and capable and able to plan such a thing in the first place, plan it for this late in the morning?

If a part of Dante had hoped to be caught, then Scarlett was inclined to believe he hadn't done this before and hadn't really wanted to do it now. Was his behaviour a cry for help?

Even so, how to deal with such a thing? Should she step forward? Intervene? Before Scarlett could decide or announce her presence, Lorenzo spoke again.

'Trouble in here is the last thing I need right now, Dante. The last thing any of us needs.' He tugged his chef's jacket into order. 'Our new financial manager will want an accounting of every Euro that comes and goes in this kitchen. You couldn't have picked a worse time to try to steal.'

The boy looked stricken. 'If you speak with her—'

'She may be just as cold about this as her mother would be. Scarlett Gibson is Lisa Firenzi's daughter. Don't think for a moment that Scarlett isn't equally capable of the same level of business-minded lack of emotion.' He drew a breath. 'I don't know if I can protect you from where Scarlett might want to take this.'

Until then the boy had still maintained a small amount of youthful expectation that the 'real grown-up'—in this case, Lorenzo—would be able to fix this for him. That expectation faded to outright concern now.

In tandem with Dante's reaction, anger inside Scarlett began to bubble up. So she was the ogre of the piece now? The one who could single-handedly destroy this boy, who clearly simply needed someone to help him get back on a straight path?

Scarlett would have Lorenzo know that she had...

Never dealt with anything quite like this.

Scarlett drew a deep breath, but it still didn't help her to dispense with the tight ache in the middle of her chest that had come from Lorenzo saying she was cold.

Could he really believe Scarlett could have no feelings for those around her?

Scarlett's hand crept up to touch her ribbon, to let her fingers absorb its soft feel.

She wasn't like that. Not really. Not deep down inside herself, and Lorenzo had known her well enough to know that. Scarlett hated that this man still had the power to cause her hurt. She'd healed from that. She'd moved on whether she now happened to be back in his actual realm of existence, or not.

'You won't get another warning.' Lorenzo glared at the boy. 'I won't discuss this with Scarlett at this stage, but don't break the rules here again. Do I make myself clear?'

'Yes. We're clear. I'm sorry.'

'You've got a chance to straighten yourself out, Dante. Don't mess it up, okay?' Lorenzo reached out to lay his hand on the boy's shoulder.

They'd both turned as they spoke, so Scarlett clearly saw the flinch, quickly disguised as a shrug when Lorenzo's hand landed on the boy's shoulder.

What—?

'You're bruised. What happened?' Lorenzo's brows drew down as his gaze examined Dante's shoulder where his shirt had pulled open a little.

And Lorenzo's expression was really odd. His face had paled. He looked sick. He had an expression in his eyes that Scarlett had…seen before? Why did that expression look like concern…and some kind of shame?

'I went mountain cycling. I fell off.' The boy uttered the words in a rapid stream as he tugged his shirt back into place. 'On the weekend. I fell into a bush.'

The words were so clearly a lie. But…why?

Lorenzo's eyes narrowed before he hurriedly rearranged his face into a mask of agreement. 'Injuries can happen in all sorts of ways.'

Like Lorenzo getting bruised and scratched falling from his motorcycle. He hadn't owned it long when Scarlett met him, and he'd told her while they were seeing each other that he'd taken several spills.

But Dante—Dante was hiding some kind of physical damage that he didn't want to tell the truth about, that *hadn't* happened riding his bike in the mountains.

Dante was unhappy at home suddenly. Unhappy enough that he'd resorted to stealing with the intention of drinking his unhappiness away?

Was Lorenzo thinking what Scarlett was thinking? Was that why Lorenzo looked sick to his heart?

'You're growing up, Dante.' Lorenzo said this with a careful air of mild interest. 'Maybe you should think about moving out of home, spread your wings a little, eh?' He forced a laugh. 'You might meet a nice girl. You won't want to have your mamma looking over your shoulder when you do that.' He drew a breath. 'In fact, I know of a woman who takes in boarders. If they're willing to help her out around the place she'll board them cheaply.'

'I'd be interested, if I could afford it.' The boy all but jumped on the suggestion. 'If she didn't want too much.'

Lorenzo shrugged as though he'd already lost most of his

interest in the topic. 'She's always up early. You could see her now, before you have to come back for your shift later.'

Dante nodded. 'Yes, that would be good, if I could see her now.'

'I'll write the name and address down for you.' Lorenzo walked to the bench and took an order pad and stub of pencil and started to scribble on it.

Scarlett realised her presence would be noted very soon if she didn't move. It was too late to disappear so her best bet was to pretend she was just arriving. She gave the door a push behind her and allowed it to bump against her back.

A couple of noisy steps forward and both their heads turned. Chirpiness was beyond her. Lorenzo's hurtful words still echoed inside her, as did concern for Dante. *Scarlett* felt sick, too. If Dante was being abused, that was a terrible thing.

'Lorenzo.' She nodded towards Dante, too, but for his sake didn't make any attempt at eye contact before she turned back to the head chef.

'I just thought I'd let you know my plans for today. I want to observe, speak with employees as I see fit, and start my study of the account books.' There would be times they would have to liaise, but Scarlett had made the decision in the past few minutes to ensure those times were kept to the absolute minimum.

Let Lorenzo think she was cold and emotionless and say 'just like her mother'. Scarlett knew her heart. She wasn't about to let Lorenzo stomp all over it, though! 'Please ensure any receipts, requisitions forms and any other money-related paperwork you might have lying around is delivered to my office. Can you do that before noon?'

She'd intended to apologise for yesterday's assumptions about his work commitments. A concession to his need for time was the closest he would now get.

Lorenzo's gaze locked on her face and searched her eyes, her expression. Scarlett knew what he would see. She'd seen it enough times herself in a mirror. A somewhat different version of Lisa's facial features in full chill-mode. How else could she protect herself?

Scarlett heaved a deep breath and slowly released it.

'I'll bring you everything I have.' Lorenzo handed the written note to Dante, but his gaze didn't leave Scarlett's face. 'Did you hear—?'

'Thank you. I've only just arrived but I really need to get to work so I hope you'll understand if I don't hang about right now. Excuse me.' She walked away before Lorenzo could do a thing about it. Not that she wanted to speak to the man now.

He might have helped Dante, and Scarlett was genuinely glad this had happened. By the sounds of it the boy needed all the help he could get.

But Lorenzo had also said some cutting things about Scarlett's personality in the process.

She didn't feel like dwelling on that, or discussing it, or anything else other than getting on with the job here and ignoring the existence of one Lorenzo Nesta and his capacity to upset her.

He shouldn't even possess that capacity.

Not at all any more!

CHAPTER THREE

'THANK you all for staying back for this meeting.' Scarlett uttered the words and let her gaze travel over each of the employees present. It was the end of her second day at Rosa's restaurant. The dinner hour was over, tables and chairs stacked, the kitchen clean and tidy. For the next few minutes it would be the site of their meeting.

Scarlett's office was not tidy. It was covered with bookwork, sheaves of account invoices and receipts. Amongst it were Lorenzo's records of kitchen expenditure. He was very thorough, and in fact so far his bookkeeping was the easiest to understand of all of this.

When Lorenzo had delivered his bookkeeping records to the office, he'd apologised for his words about her that morning. He'd clearly figured out she'd been standing there, had heard it all. He'd explained he'd wanted to scare the boy into behaving better but not make him feel as if he didn't have a friend in Lorenzo if he needed one.

Scarlett had...admired him for that and realised he hadn't been out to hurt her feelings with his words. She'd suggested the police needed to be called in to try to make sure the mother was safe. Lorenzo had surprised her with his wisdom in the matter.

Let Dante get out of there first. Once he's safe, I will make the call to the police myself. I'll ask them to check on Dante's

*mother when they're certain the boyfriend won't be around,
though it's quite possible he isn't harming her.*

He had seemed extremely uncomfortable with the topic.

Well, this understanding man was part of the Lorenzo
Scarlett had known and…

Scarlett reached behind her and twisted her hair ribbon
through her ponytail before she forced her hand back to her
side. What she'd felt or hadn't felt about Lorenzo in the past
was irrelevant now.

'I know it's late and I'm sure you'd all rather be at home
now so I'll keep this as brief as possible.' When she felt certain
she had the absolute attention of everyone there, she went on.
'I'll repeat this meeting with the remaining staff tomorrow.'

Scarlett reached for a small sheaf of papers on the bench
and handed it to the nearest person. 'If you'd take one of those
and pass the rest down the line?'

While her printouts circulated, Scarlett drew a breath and
squared her shoulders. Her gaze, whether she wanted it to or
not, shifted to Lorenzo. He stood right at the end of the group
and was the last to receive his copy of her printout.

Why did he get to look not even slightly dishevelled after
a long shift at work? And why was she noticing how Lorenzo
looked anyway?

'Everyone, what you have in your hands is a new streamlined roster, and two pages outlining expectations of you as
a staff member of Rosa.' From her discussions today with
Isabella, Scarlett suspected much of the necessity for change
in these areas came down to Luca being too lenient in certain
respects.

In the end, the how of it didn't really matter. Scarlett had
Luca's agreement that she was to set things straight here, and
she would.

Her gaze fell briefly on Dante. She wished the boy *had*
got his bruises falling off his bicycle, as Lorenzo had done

taking spills from his motorcycle years ago. At least Lorenzo had worked out Dante's problem. He'd done his best to give Dante a lifeline without harming the boy's pride. That had been kind.

You mustn't soften towards Lorenzo just because of that act of kindness. He's still a love rat.

'Work conditions, pay conditions, holidays and negotiation of time off in this establishment have all been extremely generous to this point.' Scarlett made a concerted effort to keep her thoughts on the task at hand. 'The conditions have been far more generous than the accepted norm in restaurants in this country.'

If there'd ever been written employment contracts Scarlett hadn't been able to find them. She suspected Luca would have made verbal arrangements and felt those were enough. Only by studying the rosters and what people were getting paid for hours of work, what paid holidays they received and so on, had Scarlett pieced together that her uncle had indeed been giving away too much too easily around here in his commitment to 'treating his staff well'.

Lorenzo seemed to be the only one who worked properly for his entitlements, and, in his case, he kept meticulous time sheets and never asked for overtime despite working longer hours than his weekly wage suggested he should. Since starting here four months ago he'd yet to take any extra day off that he wasn't fully entitled to.

Muttering started from a few people as they looked at the rosters.

Scarlett had expected that, but it was best to make these changes now rather than later. They wouldn't salvage Rosa in and of themselves, but they were one step in the right direction at least. 'I'd encourage you to take your handouts home and examine them. I'm certain when you do that, you'll see that the conditions are on a par—'

'This roster means I have to start an hour earlier.' The woman who made the comment spoke over Scarlett's words. She was a waitress who worked lunch shifts only. Late thirties, with high-school-aged children and a husband who ran a small farming concern not far out of Monta Correnti.

The woman turned to Lorenzo. 'It doesn't suit me to be here earlier. I have to do my housework after the family leaves for school and work each day. When *you* tried to change this, Luca said—'

'Excuse me.' Scarlett said the words firmly and waited for the woman to glance her way. 'I recall speaking with you earlier today. In fact, I've spoken with each and every staff member, explained my presence here and let you all know that, for the extent of my stay, Luca has handed the reins of control of Rosa to me.'

Did this woman think she could turn to Lorenzo and usurp Scarlett's authority? It sounded as though she'd already used Luca's generous outlook to undermine *Lorenzo's* authority, too.

That can't have been easy on the head chef, Scarlett admitted silently. She held the woman's gaze. 'I am your boss now and, while you are always welcome to discuss any concerns with our head chef in his role as Assistant Manager, it's not appropriate to do so as you've just done, ignoring my authority in the process.'

'Well, I merely wanted—'

'Miss Gibson is quite right.' Lorenzo seemed to be having his own battle. His fingers were clenched about the copy of the paperwork he'd received as his gaze took in the small group of faces. 'If changes need to be made here, perhaps it's best to be grateful that you still have a job. I've only been made aware of these changes now, as you all have, but, at first glance at least, they still seem fair and equitable to me.'

His eyes gentled as he looked at the other woman. 'Perhaps

you can rearrange your schedule so you clean your home after your shift instead of before it.'

When the woman looked ready to argue again, Scarlett spoke. What was her name? 'Maria, I'm sorry, but it doesn't suit Rosa to have one of the wait staff arriving to start a lunch shift when everyone else is run off their feet already and your presence was needed an hour earlier. Are there special circumstances for why you absolutely can't make it earlier?'

The woman dropped her gaze and muttered beneath her breath, but eventually shook her head.

'All right.' Scarlett let her gaze travel over the group. 'Across the board I've streamlined the rosters to maximise staff availability at the busiest times of the day. As staff are paid on a Thursday, this new roster will start straight after pay day, this Friday.'

She drew a breath. 'Within the next week we'll be getting ourselves up to date with written employment contracts for all staff members. It's in your best interests, as well as Rosa's, to have these in place so you know things will have to go through due process if there are ever problems.

'You'll all see that I've made it part of your conditions here that you don't try to swap rosters at the last minute unless there's a case of genuine emergency. Those will be assessed if and when they arise. Rosa will function best if we run a tight show.'

That about covered the roster side of it. 'Please read the written conditions. You'll be expected to adhere to those from now on. Cuts in the number of paid holidays et cetera simply bring Rosa into line with industry standards.'

Scarlett wound the meeting up. 'If any of you wish to discuss any aspect of the new conditions after you've read them, you are most welcome to book a meeting with me to do so. Thank you, and goodnight.'

They filed out. Good staff, many of them, and possibly a

few less than great ones. Let them go to their homes, read the conditions, take the time to absorb them and hopefully realise they were, indeed, quite reasonable.

Lorenzo was the one person who didn't file out with the others. 'That was unexpected.'

Scarlett drew a breath. 'These steps have to be taken. I thought you understood that.'

'Of course.' He spread his hands. 'As your assistant manager, I could have supported your cause better if I'd known your plans. That's all.'

Scarlett had forged ahead without consulting him or asking for his support. She admitted this. Emotionally, she didn't trust him and yet, when it came to Rosa, Isabella trusted Lorenzo. Luca trusted Lorenzo. The other staff seemed to trust Lorenzo. *Could he be* a wonderfully supportive assistant manager to Scarlett? Could they work together like that, despite their past history?

'I will try to keep that in mind in future.' In this moment, that was the best she could come up with.

Tomorrow. She would force herself to totally assess all of this tomorrow. Scarlett cast a longing glance at the door. 'It's, um, it's getting late. We should be going.'

Scarlett needed to go, so she could stop being aware of the fact that they were here alone. Alone, together, for the first time in five years. She was pushing that knowledge down as hard as she could, but it was still there.

Why couldn't she simply respond to him in the same way she responded to anyone? *Only* treat him as a co-worker. Her tummy was suddenly in knots and…

'I'll walk you to your bedsit.'

He already knew of this? 'How do you know—?'

'This is Monta Correnti.' He gestured to the restaurant. 'And this is Rosa, which is owned by Luca, who is a member of your family, which makes your presence here the topic of a great deal of interest amongst staff and patrons alike. Did you think the news that you'd moved out of Lisa's villa and into your bedsit wouldn't travel all through the restaurant in minutes?'

He shook his head. 'All the family gets talked about here, Scarlett. A week ago, it might have been "The Angel of New York's" baseball career, but your presence gets its degree of attention, too.'

Scarlett had not as yet met Luca's sons, Alex and Angelo, born to an American woman. Her Italian family certainly knew how to keep life complicated, though Scarlett wasn't at all sure that *she* wanted any time under the Rosa staff's microscope!

'Actually, I hadn't thought that news would travel through the restaurant at all.' She tugged so hard on her ribbon that it came out in her hand. Scarlett compulsively threaded it through her fingers and decided it wasn't fair that she had dressed for success and got through a *big* day, only to be startled by the strength of the gossip mill right at the end of it.

'Your nose is scrunching,' he said softly. This observation was followed by a frown that seemed self-repressive before he quickly turned his gaze away and headed for the door. 'It's less than five minutes' walk to your bedsit. I'm sure you can deal with my company for that long, despite your efforts to avoid me today.'

'I did not.' She had, though, and why did a tingle go over Scarlett's skin and her breath catch in her throat at the thought of him walking her home, for goodness' sake? 'As for moving to the bedsit, it's not that I wasn't happy at Mamma's villa.'

'Happy to the degree that you chose to move yourself into a bedsit after just two days there? And that was with your mother not even in residence in her home at the time.' He shook his head. 'You left her at age twelve, preferring to move to the other side of the world and live with your father, Scarlett. I haven't forgotten that you told me that, or of your inability to feel close to her.'

He hesitated. 'I also hear plenty about Lisa in terms of her ownership of Sorella. Your mother's restaurant is our key rival for business here.'

'Well, at least this way I avoid any conflict of interest.' Scarlett dropped her guard a little. 'I'm sure Mum would understand. Working for Luca, I couldn't allow that. Really, I should have thought of it before I came over here.'

'Certainly. I'm sure your mother should understand this.' A twinkle in his eyes showed that he could see the strategy in Scarlett's outlook. A moment later his smile faded to a more serious expression. 'Scarlett, this morning I said things about you—'

'It's all right. You explained why you made me the ogre of the piece.'

He shook his head. 'I could have thought of a better way to handle that. Realising Dante's situation…threw me off. Enough that it took all my attention to not let him know what I'd worked out.'

'You allowed him to keep his pride.'

'Sometimes pride is all a man has left.' The moment the words emerged, he clamped his lips together.

There were shadows in the backs of Lorenzo's eyes as Scarlett searched them. But he quickly shielded those eyes with long silky lashes.

'Will Dante be able to move into that boarding accommodation?' She needed to focus on that, not on her rising consciousness of Lorenzo.

Anyway, it had to be a 'workers co-operating for the better good' kind of affinity that Scarlett was feeling. Anything else would be quite insane.

Lorenzo nodded. 'He did so this morning.'

'That's good.' Scarlett glanced behind her to make absolutely sure they truly were alone. 'I can get alongside him; watch him for a while to make sure he's okay. That that horrid man, whoever he is, isn't still—'

'You don't have to worry about that. I'll keep a close watch on Dante.' Oh, his voice was so deep, so soft.

As was the expression in his eyes as he looked at her. Out of nowhere a sense of affinity rose between them. Scarlett opened her mouth and spoke straight out of that fellow feeling. 'I trust you to do that.'

She realised that she did. Without any hesitation, she knew she could trust Lorenzo with that. He might have hurt her, let her down five years ago, but she just knew this.

He's a good head chef, Scarlett. Isabella had said this.

When Luca discussed Lorenzo, he'd gone even further. *I have great faith in him.*

Maybe it was the faith of Isabella and Luca that gave Scarlett this belief in Lorenzo. Or maybe it was what she had seen of his work practices and ethics in the past two days. But they didn't seem to compute with the 'love rat' image Scarlett had carried of him for the past five years.

As Scarlett really didn't know how to address these thoughts, she turned her attention elsewhere. 'You said this morning that Dante had taken a key that Luca kept as a spare? That Dante used that to let himself into the restaurant?'

'Yes. Luca had a secret hiding place where he kept a spare key in case he ever lost his.' Lorenzo drew a key chain from the pocket of his chef's pants. There were two matching keys on it. 'I knew about it, but I thought Isabella and I were the only ones aside from Luca who did. I should have thought better of that assumption.'

He shook his head. 'In any case, that hiding place is no more. Would you like the second key?'

'No, I have one from my uncle.' Luca *had* run Rosa with

a naive degree of trust in some respects. This became more and more clear to Scarlett the more she learned about the restaurant.

'Then perhaps we should go.' Lorenzo uttered the words quietly.

'Yes.' Scarlett glanced up. The expression in Lorenzo's eyes made her breath catch in her throat.

Awareness, consciousness, memory. They were all there and for one brief moment they were all inside her, too. The feelings were so unexpected, and so opposite to what Scarlett had believed she felt towards him for five years, that she froze.

He drew a breath and stilled for a moment too before he blinked and got his feet moving and led the way to the kitchen doors. He pushed one open and stood back for her to precede him.

Somehow they made it outside and somehow she managed to say something about work as they headed across the square towards her bedsit. Her landlady had told her she travelled a lot, which suited Scarlett just fine. 'I hope the staff will realise they're not being given unreasonable conditions with the changes I've handed to them tonight.'

'If you continue to make and implement all your decisions without informing me before you put them into action, you'll make your job here harder than it needs to be.' His words were a soft murmur as his gaze travelled once again over her face, her eyes, and dropped...to her mouth before he gave an almost imperceptible shake of his head.

Scarlett forced herself to breathe carefully and evenly and not allow herself the same examination he had just taken. 'You feel that, as Head Chef and Manager, we should join our forces more?'

She had wished she could avoid him as much as she possibly could for the duration, but even Scarlett could admit that wasn't very practical when he was her assistant, and the most pivotal employee of Rosa.

'I don't want to usurp your authority here, but, yes, I do feel we need to work together.' His expression told her he wanted co-operation between them. 'I believe your likelihood of success will be better if we combine our efforts.'

He held out one hand, palm up. 'We would present a united front to the rest of the staff, if nothing else.'

'It *would* make for smoother sailing, provided you can accept my—' Authority? Her being further up the employment ladder than him? Scarlett didn't quite know how to put it, and she'd never worried about that kind of thing before!

'Provided I can accept your leadership in this workplace.' He turned, just a little turn towards her, but it made the difference between two people talking from their safe distances as they faced forwards and walked, and something just that little bit more intimate.

Scarlett doubted he was even aware he'd done it, and she could have taken one step away from him in any direction to put an end to that feeling, but instead she continued to walk exactly as close as she was to him.

Scarlett shoved her ribbon into the pocket of her dress and told herself to get over it.

Whatever *it* was, exactly.

Well, she supposed 'it' was this strange feeling she had that felt like a combination of history and remembering and becoming conscious of Lorenzo all over again in ways she hadn't anticipated and didn't welcome.

Except that no matter how much you tell yourself you're not, there's a part of you that is *aware of him.*

'I'm prepared to discuss things with you, but my decisions about the finances here are still final, no matter whether you agree with them or not.' Even so saying, she felt the need to temper her statement. 'I can see that two heads might be better than one with some of this. I suppose we can at least try.'

She had to do what was best for Rosa. If she felt this was best, such a decision didn't have to feel dangerous to Scarlett, dangerous to her emotional well-being. She wasn't about to fall in love with Lorenzo again, for crying out loud. They could work side by side for the betterment of Rosa. In fact, doing so would be really good for her because it would prove to her that she could remain completely emotionally distanced from him.

And physical attraction, Scarlett?

These few moments this evening of feeling a little too conscious of him, well, they were probably just a couple of old memories surfacing. They didn't mean anything and would be long gone and forgotten by tomorrow morning when she met him again at work.

Scarlett drew a breath that filled her lungs with the blunted scent of his aftershave lotion and realised they were somehow walking even closer than they had been. Their shoulders were leaning towards each other. He smelled familiar and...she was far too tired for this right now. Her defences were not as strong as they should be.

'Thank you. I want to help you, Scarlett, not get in the way of what you're trying to do here.' Lorenzo drew a deep breath.

They arrived at her bedsit and stepped into the lee of the door lintel.

'Goodnight—'

'Thank you for seeing me—'

He reached for her hand, perhaps to shake it.

Scarlett took a step towards the door as he did so, and they each stepped into the other's path. Lorenzo's hands came up to cup her elbows, perhaps to hold her still while he stepped around her.

Instead she glanced up. He glanced down into her eyes and a moment later, their lips met.

CHAPTER FOUR

'GOODNIGHT. I—thank you for seeing me home.' Scarlett uttered the words through lips that wanted to deny what had just happened.

Wanted to deny a kiss that had lasted less than a second, a mere brush of lips against lips before she and Lorenzo had both...broken away. They'd each stepped back as though they'd been burnt. 'I have to—'

She couldn't make calm words come out, couldn't do anything to downplay something that shouldn't even need to be downplayed and yet, to Scarlett, the entire world had stopped and then started up again and now it was spinning strangely and nothing felt quite right because of Lorenzo's kiss...

Barely even a kiss, Scarlett.

Somehow she got her key straight into the lock, twisted it and got the door open. Her feet carried her through and she closed the door. She didn't look back, and then through the closed door she heard his footsteps taking him away in a rapid stride that went, and then half missed a step, and then kept going.

He'd hesitated.

And as that happened Scarlett had leaned her shoulder against the closed door and shut her eyes and silently willed... What? For him to stop? Keep walking away?

She should have said something. Scarlett shouldn't have

allowed that kiss to happen in the first place. And that was the problem. Scarlett didn't believe either one of them had anticipated the kiss happening. It hadn't been planned or thought about. How could she protect against the possibility of something she simply hadn't expected?

For one little blink in time, five years had dropped away and they'd simply reached for each other. That should not, even for a second, have seemed the natural thing to do.

This had shocked her.

Perhaps it had also shocked Lorenzo.

Then maybe you should ask yourself how it's affected you now that it's happened?

Scarlett shook her head and went to the wardrobe to pull out her workout clothes of knee-length fitted black pants and lime-green vest-top and trainers. She clipped on her iPod, turned the music to a mind-numbing set, and began her Pilates routine.

Forget being kissed by a man who had no right to kiss her, before they both realised the insanity of their actions, and stopped. Forget how it had happened or why it had happened or anything else about it.

Scarlett was here for Rosa and her family and she only wanted to think about those issues. She forced her brain to the tricky issue of pulling Rosa into an utterly profitable financial position, and kept her thoughts there as she stretched and twisted and limbered away the tensions of her day.

Over the next five days, Scarlett forced aside what she chose to refer to in her thoughts when she couldn't avoid acknowledging it altogether, as 'that regrettable moment'. And indeed for the most part, she did a very good job of forgetting/ignoring/not confronting the issue in a tizzy of busyness at the restaurant.

She worked hard, visited often with Isabella and sometimes

with other family members. She also co-operated with Lorenzo in terms of the running of Rosa where that co-operation was needed, and he co-operated with her. Scarlett felt quite certain that Lorenzo also didn't give the matter of that one, tiny, completely insignificant slip that had occurred outside her bedsit a single thought.

She frowned and dipped her hand through the cool, clear swimming pool water. Today was Monday and the restaurant was closed during the main part of the day while the town observed a partial religious holiday. For those so inclined there'd been church services earlier. Rosa would staff up at four p.m. and open for business for the evening.

For now, Scarlett, Isabella and Scarlett's sister Jackie were lazing in this sheltered swimming pool that was available to townsfolk who belonged either as students or teachers to the study faculty that owned it. It was a hot day, and quiet and restful here. Getting away for this had been a very welcome idea.

Scarlett dipped her shoulders beneath the cool water. Her hair was up in an untidy knot on top of her head, secured with a hair band and a thick red ribbon that exactly matched her high-cut one-piece red suit. She was *not* obsessive-compulsive about her ribbons. Scarlett simply enjoyed finding new ones and matching them to her clothing.

Lorenzo has looked at each change of ribbon. His gaze goes often to your hair. He used to enjoy sifting it through his fingers…

Oh! Scarlett pinched her lips together. She was having a rest. Thinking about the head chef of Rosa was not on her agenda for right now. For at all! She turned to Jackie and forced a smile. 'This *is* nice. Thanks for talking me into joining you and Izzie.'

'You've been hard to pin down for any one-on-one time since you came back to Monta Correnti.' Jackie's words were not accusatory, simply honest. 'When Romano said he needed to come out here, I thought why not make a little pool party of it?'

Had Jackie chosen an event where Isabella would be present to make this a little easier for her sister? Scarlett didn't know what to say. Of all the family, Jackie was the one she found it most difficult to spend time with.

Her guilt over her sister's loss of her daughter, Kate, for so many years ate at her. Scarlett…didn't know how to deal with that. And she realised now, as she looked into Jackie's eyes, that she had been avoiding her sister *because* of this issue.

Before Scarlett could speak, and she didn't know what she would have said anyway, Jackie went on.

'Romano had to come out here anyway for a meeting. He only teaches an evening class once a week, but now that he's on the board of teachers things like that come up periodically.' Her voice softened as she spoke of the man who'd been her teenage lover and also the father of the baby that Jackie had given up for adoption. 'I figured we'd all be grateful for some time in the water, anyway.'

That was true. It was a hot day.

'Do you suppose we should actually make some appearance of swimming, just so we look like we belong in here?' Isabella asked the question without moving a muscle.

'Oh, I think somnolent suits us fairly well, don't you?' Scarlett inserted this quip and was proud of her effort. She wanted…to feel closer to Jackie, and to feel comfortable with her sister overall. That would be nice, but it wasn't going to happen while Scarlett kept putting off self-protective prickle vibes every time they were near each other.

Isabella seemed to have dealt with any guilt that she felt over Jackie's loss. Why couldn't Scarlett do the same and put all that behind her?

'Well, I'm not moving an inch until Romano finishes his

meeting with the others and comes to join us.' Jackie laughed and settled her arms more firmly back against the edge of the pool.

Isabella raised her brows in Scarlett's direction. 'You never said what the phone call was about from your mother yesterday at the restaurant, Scarlett. Is it anything I should know about, or tell Papa? I know we've put you in charge but I wouldn't want you to think you have to deal with everything all by yourself. If there are any issues with Sorella—'

'No, it wasn't about either of the restaurants.' Her mother and her uncle Luca owned a restaurant each. Their rivalry when it came to those restaurants was long-standing, though from the viewpoint of the staff actually working at Rosa, at least, Scarlett wasn't really picking up that vibe. They just wanted to get on with the job. It wouldn't surprise her too much to learn that the staff at Sorella felt the same way.

'As predicted, Izzie, Mamma wasn't happy to know that I'd moved out of her home.' Scarlett shrugged. 'She wasn't pleased initially to know that I was going to work at Rosa, either. I thought, when she invited me to stay at her villa while I was here, that she'd got over that.'

'I wish she and my father could just get along.' Isabella shook her head. 'I hope her call didn't upset you too much, Scarlett.'

'No. That's just Mamma. Her reaction just concreted it in for me that I'd made the right decision in moving out of her villa.' Scarlett let her glance encompass Jackie. 'As for my working at Rosa, that's my decision. It's got nothing to do with our mother.'

Jackie dipped her chin in acknowledgement. 'That sounds very fair to me.'

It was. And Scarlett appreciated the support. 'Mamma said that Elizabeth would never move out of her own mother's home making the entire town assume that home wasn't good enough for her.'

Jackie stared for a moment and then threw her head back and laughed.

Scarlett shook her head in bewilderment. 'What?'

'Lizzie might be the one of us who gets on the best with our mother, but Lizzie is also *living in Australia!* It's not as though she's right in Mamma's pocket all the time to test the friendship, so to speak.' Jackie's smile widened. 'It's just that *you're the one* who looks exactly like Mamma when you pull that intolerant, fed-up-to-the-gills expression.'

'Oh, thanks very much!' Scarlett flicked water at her sister and received the same treatment back.

Izzie, caught in the middle, squealed and ducked right under the water, which somewhat defeated the purpose if she'd been trying to avoid being splashed.

Scarlett and Jackie grinned at each other over Izzie's head as she resurfaced, and Scarlett's grin faded as that inexplicable ache started up in her chest again. She forced the smile to return and said as lightly as she could manage, 'I spent a little time getting to know Lizzie better over the past few months. We exchanged some emails and spent some time together in Melbourne one weekend.'

Scarlett and her eldest sister had sort of bonded. 'I wish I'd connected with her a lot sooner. We were both living in Australia. It would have been nice—' She broke off, not wanting to make Jackie feel left out.

When she searched her sister's face, Scarlett couldn't help but comment on something else she'd noticed about Jackie. '*You* have a real glow about you, Jackie. Every time you fall silent your face gets this soft look.'

It was as though when her sister disappeared inside her own thoughts, whatever she found in there lit her up like a thousand candles all burning at once.

'Romano's a big part of the reason for that, of course.' Jackie's smile was indeed soft and glowing as she spoke of him, but it wasn't…all that Scarlett had seen in her sister.

'But Romano tells me the same thing any time I've been to visit with our daughter or we've had her over to spend time with us.' Jackie's mouth softened and love and happiness poured out of her. 'We know we can't take the place of the parents who've raised her. We wouldn't try. We're thrilled that Kate has been happy!

'But Kate has such a generous heart. She's let us in, let us be a second set of people who love her. I'm so happy to finally have even a "piece" of my daughter. The only problem is one of her sets of adopted grandparents. They're having a hard time accepting me, or Romano, as part of Kate's life.'

A fierce expression crossed Jackie's face. 'I wouldn't trade anything for having Kate back in my life, and just let anyone try to get in the way of that. I'm being polite but if anyone messed this up for me now and somehow took Kate out of my life again, I'd never forgive it.'

She cast a horrified glance at Scarlett. 'I didn't mean that to sound as though I can't—'

Forgive Scarlett for taking Kate out of her life?

'It's all right.' Scarlett's tummy twisted. 'I understand what you meant.'

But why shouldn't Jackie be angry anyway? And stay that way for as long as she wanted? Maybe never truly be able to forgive Scarlett way deep down where it mattered? Scarlett was the one whom Jackie had entrusted many years ago with a letter to Romano telling him about her pregnancy. And Scarlett had let that letter go into the river and never told…

Jackie bit her lip. 'I'm so happy. A part of me sometimes fears I could lose it all again. It's just that I don't think I could cope with that.'

'It won't happen, Jackie. Of course it won't.' It was Izzie

who reached out and took Jackie's hand, who held it and seemed able to keep Jackie's words in some kind of perspective that Scarlett, in this moment, tried to but couldn't.

All Scarlett could do was feel her sister's loss, deep down inside her soul, and acknowledge that loss was her, *Scarlett's*, fault. She'd run from truly acknowledging that for a long time.

Izzie went on. 'Kate loves you way too much to let that happen. You have to remember she's a grown-up girl with a mind of her own, just like you.'

Jackie shook her head as though to shake the dark thoughts away. 'I know. I get silly over it sometimes, too protective of what I've been given back, I guess.'

Izzie nodded. 'And you've had a lot of emotional ground to cover, getting back together with Romano after all this time as well, him learning of Kate's existence.'

And Jackie having to deal with being told that Scarlett and Izzie had caused all those barren years in her life by throwing her letter away that day instead of delivering it as Jackie had asked Scarlett to do.

A part of Scarlett wanted, quite desperately, to climb out of the swimming pool, claim some urgent and only just remembered prior engagement or something, and…run away. But she'd done that once already, had run all the way to Australia.

She'd gone to see her father. To get to know her father.

No, Scarlett. You ran away from the emotional upheaval of what you'd done. Getting to know Dad, being loved by him, was an unanticipated bonus.

'I've got some lovely photos of Kate, Scarlett.' Animation swept back into Jackie's face as she said this.

Beyond them, the door of the nearest building swung open and a small group of men stepped out. Scarlett's glance caught on one of them, half hidden from her view behind the others.

She was dreaming up Lorenzo's presence everywhere. Just because whoever that was was dark-haired and had a slender build and looked about the same height. Oh, maybe she just felt too overwhelmed in too many ways at the moment. And she couldn't just ignore what Jackie had said.

Scarlett had to stop this nonsense, otherwise Jackie might start to think she wasn't happy for her and that truly would be awful. 'Izzie mentioned that you'd got some great photos of–of—Kate.'

'I'd like you to see them.' Jackie's eyes softened. 'At least that way you can start to feel as though you know her a little. Do you know, I can see Romano in her eyes and the shape of her nose.'

Jackie went on, enthusing about her daughter's physical features. To hear Jackie tell it, her daughter was the most beautiful girl ever to exist.

It hurt Scarlett to hear it, even though it made her happy for Jackie, too. 'I'd…love to see the photos, Jackie.' What else could she say?

'I'll put a CD together for you.' Jackie glanced towards the approaching men and raised her voice. 'Romano. Come swim!' She started to swim towards the other end of the pool to greet the love of her life.

Izzie laid her hand on Scarlett's arm. 'Are you okay, Scarlett? Jackie's fine, you know. She's bound to have these moments, but you heard her. Her life is so happy overall.'

'I can see that.' And Scarlett was happy for Jackie for that. Of course she was. 'But she's also dealing with old grief, and with feelings about family that you and I can only try to understand. She's got a very generous heart, to be able or even willing to brush aside my part in all that the way she is.'

'And mine.' Isabella's face tightened. 'I was as much to blame.'

'Not really. I'm the one Jackie entrusted that letter to.'

Isabella drew a breath and the tension faded from her face. She raised her arm to wave. 'Lorenzo, I didn't know you were out here. Come join us.'

Scarlett froze. She wanted to look, but she didn't want him to know that she was interested.

Excuse me, you're not *interested!*

But Scarlett turned her head just as there was a quiet splash. And there was Lorenzo slicing through the water towards them. Vaguely, Scarlett registered Romano and Jackie and another man in the water at the other end of the pool, talking. And Isabella talking.

'We should do this more often, Scarlett. I could talk to Jackie about another visit here.' Isabella's voice went on.

But Scarlett wasn't really listening. And all she could see was Lorenzo. Bare-chested, his lithe body slicing through the water as he moved with neat strokes until he surfaced at their end of the pool, a little to Isabella's left.

He seemed…more comfortable with his body nowadays. Maybe maturity had brought that to him? Because back then he'd never liked to swim publicly, or even take his shirt off in front of others. He'd hated Scarlett to even see it if he'd had one of his spills and had a bruise or a scratch. At other times he'd been fine…

'Scarlett? Did you hear me?' Izzie asked the question in a puzzled tone.

What her cousin might have said prior to that, well, actually Scarlett had no idea. 'Sorry, Izzie?' Scarlett dredged her mind. 'Oh, yes, it would be fun to come here again.' The pool was shaded with beautiful trees and the whole complex was set halfway up a quiet hillside with a beautiful view over a lush green valley.

Scarlett had to act normally. She had already seemed quite out of it to her cousin. And she *could* be normal around Lorenzo. Of course she could. He was just a man!

He's the man you had an affair with five years ago when he was still married.

Well, yes, but Scarlett hadn't known about that until it was too late.

And she didn't have those feelings about him any more. Being in his company simply made her uneasy because of past history, that was all.

'Hello, Lorenzo.' There. You see? She sounded perfectly normal.

Scarlett's hand rose to pat at the ribbon in her hair. It got halfway to its goal before she stopped herself and let her arm fall back into the water.

It wasn't helping that Lorenzo was practically naked, and look how tanned he was, and muscular, and he *was* wearing the medallion...

'It's a lovely day for a swim.' Scarlett pushed her lips up into a very, very natural and completely relaxed and not at all overly conscious of him smile. 'Do you teach classes out here or something?'

'The board wanted to discuss that possibility with me.' His eyes were narrowed.

Against the sun, Scarlett told herself, and refused to acknowledge that his gaze had followed the movement of her hand, had tracked the rest of the way to touch on her messy knot of hair before it travelled gently over her face and bare shoulders.

'Um, well, that sounds interesting.' She glanced at her cousin, whose gaze was passing from her to Lorenzo and back again.

'With what they wanted, I'd have considered it a conflict

of interest against my work at Rosa.' He gave a shrug. 'So unfortunately I had to turn the offer down.'

'I see.' Scarlett should have thought of the possible threat to Rosa straight away.

Well, it would be nice if she could think anything beyond wanting to swim over to him and speak at a much closer level, wouldn't it? One that involved ignoring the presence of the others in the pool, and preferably allowing their lips to meet...

So much for telling herself that first kiss had been some random thing, like tripping over and falling onto his mouth or something. Maybe she should have examined that first kiss and its impact on her, rather than trying to pretend it hadn't happened. Would that have better equipped her for now?

Failing that, Scarlett had another highly appropriate plan to implement. 'I must take advantage and do some laps before we have to leave.'

She uttered the words as though to Isabella, and made an odd waving motion with one hand. 'Excuse me. Do feel free to talk amongst yourselves.'

And with this obscure blessing handed to Izzie and Lorenzo, who both probably stared after her as though she'd lost her mind at the bottom of the swimming pool, Scarlett set off to do laps.

Perhaps until she swam herself into oblivion.

At least until she would no longer be conscious of Lorenzo's presence in such an *everything-else-fades-to-black* kind of way.

Izzie wouldn't have noticed anything all that odd in Scarlett's reactions to Lorenzo, would she?

Scarlett increased her pace, churning through the water as though by doing so she might somehow escape all of her thoughts.

She decided Izzie would not have noticed, and, not only

that, Scarlett didn't have to think about anything. Not Lorenzo, not family, not her guilt over Jackie, not sending herself to Australia for years and years and then coming back here with all sorts of hopes apparently tucked away inside her like unexpected add-ons that she shouldn't have stuffed into her mental suitcases.

Stroke, breathe. Stroke, breathe.

Scarlett focused one hundred, no, *two hundred* per cent of her attention on her movements through the water.

And pushed every other distraction right out!

CHAPTER FIVE

'THERE has to be an answer somewhere. I just *know* it's there, but I can't zero in on it.' Scarlett murmured the words beneath her breath, mostly in the hopes of getting them out of her head.

Her swim earlier this afternoon felt aeons away. Night had fallen outside the restaurant while she slaved away in Luca's office inputting financial information onto a computer system to bring Rosa's paperwork side of things—kicking and screaming if necessary—into the twenty-first century.

Well, it had been a big day. Scarlett had come out onto the terrace that adjoined with Sorella's terrace for a breath of air, even if that air was still quite warm and balmy.

There was nobody out here at this time of night, and in fact, though the terraces joined, there was an air of disuse about both of them.

She had to stop this nonsense when it came to Rosa's head chef. She had to stop it *right now,* if not sooner. It just wasn't right that she still could react to him that way when he'd broken her heart, let her down so badly.

Yes, but he's also been the epitome of a fabulous head chef since you've been at Rosa. He's committed to the restaurant. You saw how wonderful he was with Dante and that whole situation. Isabella thinks the world of him.

Maybe Lorenzo had changed.

And, well, five years on…

She'd heard on the rumour-mill, during her last trip over here that the new head chef at Rosa was single, so he'd done the right thing in the end and got out of that loveless relationship. That meant he was free now.

Just what do you mean by that, Scarlett? Free for you to get involved with a second time? Are you nuts?

She wasn't crazy but Scarlett *was* still somewhat attracted to Lorenzo. That didn't have to be an issue, though!

'Here you are. I thought you might have still been holed up in Luca's office.'

Lorenzo's words were low-pitched, in tune with the quiet atmosphere out here. Scarlett's reaction was for her pulse to skip before she turned slowly to face him.

'I came out for a breath of air.' She *had* been working in Luca's office for a lot of hours.

'Well, now you can have something to refresh you at the same time. Don't worry.' He pressed one of two glasses of red wine into her hand.

Their fingers brushed as Scarlett automatically took the drink from him. She tried not to notice the warmth of his fingers, the familiarity of taking a glass from him. The quiet of the night around them or how it felt good to stand here with him, just the two of them. 'Worry?'

'About the expense.' He gestured with his glass. 'I'm not costing the restaurant money. A patron bought this whole bottle, had us uncork it, and then ended up leaving without touching it.'

'Oh. Yes. Very good. Well, thank you for the drink.' She said it rather assertively and took a sip. Scarlett would *not* reach for the ribbon in her hair. It was navy blue this evening, velvet and soft and…comforting.

Not reaching.
Don't need to feel comforted.

Doing just fine holding up all by myself.

Not tempted by Lorenzo, either.

Totally not thinking about being kissed by him and how that one brief kiss only made me want—

Nothing. Scarlett wanted nothing from Lorenzo aside from good cooking. 'I thought you'd be in the kitchen. Has the clientele eased off already?'

'Not only has it eased off, the evening is over, Scarlett.' He sipped from his own glass of wine.

'Really?' Scarlett's gaze dipped to the strong column of his neck, to the bob of his Adam's apple as he swallowed the rich red.

What was she doing? Letting herself enjoy Lorenzo's company? Lorenzo's words finally got through the fog of what she decided must be over-tiredness messing up her normal thought patterns.

Scarlett frowned. 'Has the restaurant closed?'

'Yes. It's just as well I check the building thoroughly before I leave. You might have ended up spending the night out here.' He leaned one arm against the railing that edged the terraced area. 'Did you even eat the meal I sent in to you earlier?'

'I did. Thank you.' Every day Lorenzo made sure she ate. He took care of her that way, even when she had her head down for hours and hours, like today. 'I want to get Rosa into a truly successful position and keep the restaurant there.'

'You've implemented changes, and smoothed ruffled feathers of various staff members when necessary.' He sipped his wine again. 'Bringing staff conditions into a more sensible place has to be a good start.'

'A good start, yes, but it's not going to be enough.' Working on the books had made that abundantly clear. 'We need to lift our client base and keep it lifted.' She didn't notice the change in her speech from 'I' to 'we'.

As the days passed, Lorenzo had worked quietly to support

her efforts. And somehow through that, Scarlett had started to trust him and rely on him.

Only as the head chef here. Well, as the *assistant manager* and head chef.

'I've stopped you from going home. I'm sorry. I lost track of the time.' That had happened while she turned her mind inside out trying to find a larger overall solution to Rosa's financial issues.

Now all Scarlett could register was Lorenzo's closeness. She had to pull herself together!

'Maybe you should tell me what brought you out here in the first place.' He said it as an invitation, not a challenge.

And Scarlett found herself responding. 'I have to find a way to let the general public know the true value of Rosa.' She let her gaze meet his in the dimness.

His eyes gleamed with interest in what she was saying, but there was more, too, and Scarlett went on a little breathlessly.

'There has to be a way to make Rosa stand out against a neighbour like the glitzy, internationally flavoured Sorella.' She had sent out a feeler for one idea that might help.

Scarlett would have elaborated on that.

But he chose that moment to lay his hand on her arm. 'If there is any other way I can help—I can work longer hours—'

'You already give of your time and don't claim the overtime you should.' This was also something that had bothered Scarlett. Of all the staff that Rosa employed, Lorenzo was the one who should be paid *more*.

She tried not to react to the knowledge of his hand against the bare skin of her arm, tried not to want more of his touch. Yet when he finally dropped his hand away, she missed it.

'That's not important at the moment.' He turned his head

away, almost as though her comprehending his generosity had embarrassed him.

'You—you made us some money catering to that movie star for her special lunch.' Oh, Scarlett wanted to rest *her* hand against his arm, to touch him and feel his warmth.

'Maybe we need to find a way to bring Hollywood to Rosa's front door.' He smiled a little as he said it.

'Yes, why not? We'll move the entire tinsel town here. Do you think anyone would notice it had gone missing?' Scarlett returned his smile. They fell silent and finished their wine and…he was so close. She could smell the scent of his cologne, and old memories suddenly got all tangled up with the here and now.

She dropped her gaze away from him. The goal that had been to think about the future of Rosa and see if a break from the office would rattle loose any other ideas inside her mind faded in the face of her awareness of him.

Why was Lorenzo different from any other man? Surely, lots of men could kiss her and make her feel the same way he did. Or even better. Not that Scarlett had kissed a whole lot of men in the past years, and not that any of the candidates she had kissed had stacked up.

She'd been busy building her career. For that reason she hadn't involved herself in a great amount of dating.

And so what if none of them had swept her away?

These thoughts were *not* productive, especially at this time of night when she was obviously weary and not able to think clearly.

'Has it been hard for you, Scarlett? Coming back like this?' He turned and somehow their fingers were brushing, just gently touching on the railing. 'You seemed unhappy when I first saw you today at the swimming pool with your sister and Isabella.'

'I didn't think you'd see.' What *had* he seen? She searched his gaze, and somehow in the dim quietness the words came out. 'It's no secret now, that Jackie had a daughter a long time ago. What most people wouldn't know is that I all but single-handedly separated them back then. This afternoon at the pool, when Jackie was talking about Kate, I felt guilty for the way I'd hurt her.'

Scarlett felt emotion clog her throat, and she was appalled. She shouldn't have let this out. 'You mustn't say anything to anyone. That's…'

'Your business, and Jackie's business.' He shook his head. 'I won't say anything. I…understand about secrets.'

Until he said those words, Scarlett had thought he might pull her into his arms, hold her, and perhaps try to kiss those painful emotions away.

She would have let him.

In fact, somewhere deep inside she admitted she might even have wanted that.

But his admission about secrets hung between them, a thinly veiled reference to his past marriage.

'Well, I'm being a bit dramatic all of a sudden.' Scarlett made as light of things as she could manage. 'I shouldn't have brought that old history up. Jackie just wants to forget it now that she has Kate in her life again. And, it's late. We should go in. I'm sure you'd like to leave. I'm sorry I held things up daydreaming out here.'

Scarlett turned for the inside of the restaurant. She hadn't exactly been daydreaming, but he would know what she meant.

'Yes, of course we can go.' Lorenzo looked at the tight set of Scarlett's shoulders. She had on a simple light tan sheath that looked cool and comfortable, and brought out the beauty of her bone structure and the golden glow of her skin.

That glow had been in her face, too, until he stupidly brought up her earlier unease in her sister's company.

Yet he couldn't really regret it, because Scarlett had given him a gift just now. The gift of her trust for just a few moments before her openness made her uneasy and she wished she could have taken it all back.

He had wanted to comfort her but he'd drawn back from that, too. How could he do that when the guilt of his past plagued him? The guilt of his past and…the complications of his present.

'I'll see you home.' He'd walk her over and walk away. That was all he could do with Scarlett. What else did he have to offer her? Nothing. Lorenzo was not free to offer Scarlett anything.

And of course, after all this time, he didn't still want to. It had to be their past that made it difficult for him to maintain equilibrium in his thoughts where she was concerned.

'No, thanks.' She walked ahead of him through the restaurant, glanced back over her shoulder. 'By the time you finish locking up and get on your motorcycle I'll be there. I'll be fine, Lorenzo. I don't need you to go with me.'

She left him there, and he did watch to make sure she got home safely while her words rang in his head.

They didn't need each other.

That had to be the truth of it.

Didn't it?

'You'll understand if I ask you to explain your reasoning for whatever choices you make today?' Scarlett asked the question quietly as Lorenzo drew Rosa's small van to a stop outside a set of shops in a nearby larger township.

'Of course.' Lorenzo wasn't concerned to know that Scarlett would spend this morning scrutinising his work practices. He had nothing to hide.

They were on a buying expedition, and both of them were in a mellow mood.

A cooling breeze had driven the worst of the heat away. The day was clear and fresh. It was nice to be away from the restaurant for a little while. Isabella had taken charge to free Lorenzo for his expedition. He'd climbed into the van and Scarlett had joined him so she could see what one of his buying trips consisted of. When he'd turned the key in the ignition, old rock music had blared out of the van's speakers.

Scarlett had thrown her head back and laughed and he'd... laughed with her. He'd turned the volume down a little and they'd made the trip with the windows down, the wind whipping through their hair and against their faces. It had been... fun.

Lorenzo glanced at Scarlett's flushed face, and couldn't help the soft smile that came to his lips. 'You can cross-question me all you like. I want Rosa to succeed as much as you do.'

Lorenzo got out of the van to stride around the front and open Scarlett's door with a bow and a flourish. 'Shall we go?'

For a moment she froze, but then a smile came over her face and she held out her hand and lifted her nose into the air at such a haughty angle it was a wonder it didn't catch on the top of the doorframe. 'By all means let us go, but you should know, I'm not carrying the basket for you.'

'Actually, I have string bags, and I'll be doing the carrying myself.' He gripped her hand and helped her out, and their hands slid away from each other with a slow glide of fingers.

They went shopping. Lorenzo made his choices as carefully as he always did. These were ingredients and items he couldn't get for the kitchen locally in Monta Correnti.

Scarlett observed, questioned his brand choices, and nodded her approval as he carefully explained how each item would be used.

When they'd finished the shopping for Rosa, he gestured towards another small shop. 'If you don't mind me taking the time, I'd like a few things from in there for my home stores. They can wait if you'd prefer.'

'No, that's fine.' Her eyes had lit up as she realised what they were looking at. It was a chocolate wholesaler. She turned to glance at him with her brows raised. 'I know you make fabulous desserts. You were working on some the first day I started at Rosa, but I wouldn't have pictured you with a sweet tooth for it.'

'Then picture again.' He smiled and shrugged his shoulders. 'I occasionally make them at home. Partly to keep my hand in and my capabilities sharp, but mostly—' he smiled '—so I can eat the results. Maybe one day I could cook a dessert for you.'

'Maybe.'

A little silence fell. It wasn't awkward, exactly, just both of them realising that they'd let their conversation drift into something it perhaps hadn't started out to be.

That perhaps wasn't particularly appropriate, and Lorenzo tried to remind himself of this as he gathered up his purchases and the items were tallied.

He managed, sort of. Well, except for his imagination taking him to making chocolate desserts for Scarlett and feeding portions to her somewhere quiet and romantic.

You've managed not to feel romantic about anyone else for five years.

Lorenzo hadn't been celibate, but those encounters had been occasional, and emotionally meaningless.

'Lunch.' He needed to shift his thoughts away from the concepts of Scarlett and romance. 'We, ah, we agreed that we'd eat at the most popular restaurant, check out the competition.'

'My guess would be that one.' Scarlett gestured to a small,

cosy restaurant tucked into the corner of the square. It wasn't the largest, but it was clearly busy. 'Shall we go there?'

Lorenzo tucked their purchases into coolers in the back of the van, and they made their way on foot to the restaurant.

'The demographic they're getting is different here from Rosa.' Scarlett leaned forward to say the words quietly, so they wouldn't be overheard by other diners. So no one would know they were being studied and picked apart. 'We get some tourists, but not as many as we have locals.'

To be fair, she and Lorenzo were picking apart the food, table service, ambiance and everything else as well. That was why they were here. To examine all of it.

She took a small sip of her wine. 'It's a decent red. Nothing outstanding, but I don't think you'd do better for a table-wine price.'

'Yes. The wine is good value.' Lorenzo's lids drooped and his gaze stilled on her lips.

Scarlett was trying hard not to be too aware of him, too conscious. And yet with each moment that passed, her awareness seemed to increase.

They'd laughed together this morning as they drove here. Played silly old music in the van and let themselves relax. Scarlett had let her guards down. She couldn't seem to get them back up again.

'They're catering to at least a fifty-per-cent tourist clientele here.' Lorenzo leaned in a little closer. 'These are people who *won't* be back again and again. They just want to eat and leave.'

'It can be a tricky one, the tourist versus locals issue.' Scarlett tried to give the issue the most careful thought she could manage.

That wasn't a full hundred per cent, she had to admit. How could she fully concentrate on business when all she could hear was his voice? When all she could feel was the fact he was so close she could raise her hand and touch his face?

And he was looking at her as though, regardless of their purpose here, he saw only her.

Scarlett cleared her throat. 'You, ah, with your shopping earlier—the Rosa part of it.' Yes, that was good. Rosa was what they needed to speak about, even if Scarlett now had an almost compulsive need to be in a kitchen with him somewhere and watch him create a chocolate masterpiece.

For her?

No. Of course not.

Well, it would be rather special.

I repeat, Scarlett, no, of course not!

It would not be special. It would be dangerously intimate.

'Um, where were we?'

The liquid brown of his eyes darkened as he gazed at her through a screen of silky black lashes. 'We were discussing my shopping for Rosa.'

'That's right. We were.' Scarlett forced a nod, but all that did was make her ponytail bounce and the forest-green ribbon brush against the skin of her back. A sleeveless sundress in a matching green had seemed a good choice this morning, but now Scarlett wondered if maybe she should have dressed in something more workmanlike. Well, work-womanlike, if she wanted to be exact about it.

Maybe a suit that buttoned up to the neck. With tights. Boring, sensible ones. And low-heeled pumps. And no ribbon in her hair. Definitely no ribbon from her collection of ribbons that Scarlett anticipated wearing each day now for that moment when Lorenzo let his gaze wander to her hair.

'I've studied the way you run your kitchen, Lorenzo.' She drew a breath that she hoped would help to steady her before she forced herself to go on. 'From this morning's shopping, the only noteworthy issue was that we could purchase a lot of our goods from here on a regular basis and get them for less than we're paying to local producers from Monta Correnti and its surrounds.'

His fingers lifted as though he might attempt to smooth the puckered expression from her lips, but he dropped them back to the table and instead gave a nod of agreement. 'You're quite right, but Luca's policy has been to support local business.'

'Yet recently I saw you in a heated discussion with a local olive supplier when he brought a case of olives to the restaurant.' Scarlett had meant to follow up on that, but had become immersed again in account records and, truthfully, had forgotten. She shouldn't allow issues to slip away from her that way. Everything counted!

It was Lorenzo's turn to frown. 'The olives that grower brought wouldn't be fit to put on a cheap mass-produced pizza from some foreign country that doesn't have a clue!'

Scarlett grinned. She couldn't help herself. 'Are you having a go at *my* country's food-chain pizza makers? I'm sure the last time I had an olive on one of those pizzas, it was quite satisfactory. But then, Australia produces some good olives.'

She was teasing him.

And he was looking all affronted but with a twinkle in his eyes, letting her.

Scarlett was shocked at her own behaviour, and thrilled and happy and a little giddy from his company, all at once.

Oh, she had allowed herself to relax too much with him today. That was the problem. Relax and unwind and for a little while, though the entire purpose of her presence with him was to dig into yet another aspect of Rosa's doings in hopes of finding another edge she could trim off their bottom line, she'd simply had fun.

'Why can't I still loathe you, 'Renz?' The old pet name for him slipped out without her even realising it. The question slipped out, too, straight from her confusion and interest in him. It also came from a degree of caution and the belated realisation that she really had let this day get out of her control. 'You hurt me so much.'

'That is something I have regretted every day for five years.' He didn't say that he wished he could have fixed the situation, made it better. That he wished he could have done things differently back then.

Scarlett noted that. Oh, she heard that fact loud and clear. And even then, she still couldn't.

Had she *ever* hated him? Or had she only thought that she did, because being angry had been easier to deal with than the pain of losing him? The pain of him not caring for her enough to leave his wife and give Scarlett the future with him that she had hoped for?

A future that Lorenzo had promised and then not followed through on? She hadn't known he was married at first. She'd let herself fall in love with him before he told her. He'd been going to leave Marcella. He'd done that since. Why couldn't he have done it then? 'It was a long time ago and maybe we both have grown up since then.'

Maybe growing up was what allowed Lorenzo to finally get out of a marriage that had made him unhappy. At least he'd done that for himself.

And Scarlett had moved on, too. Perhaps they just hadn't been meant to be together.

When she searched his eyes she thought she would see agreement. Perhaps softness. Maybe still that hint of teasing. She didn't expect to see shadows. Such shadows that her breath caught in her throat and she uttered his name with a question in her voice. 'Lorenzo?'

What is it? What's brought that hurt into your eyes?

He swallowed and opened his mouth and for some reason her breath stilled as though she was bracing for something.

But he just shook his head and gestured to her plate. 'Are you finished? If so we should probably make our way back. There's a lot of work still to do before the day is over.'

'Y-yes. I'm finished.' So, apparently, was this conversation if she didn't try… 'If you need—'

'I'm fine, Scarlett, but we do need to head back.' He didn't reject her care. The gentle expression in his eyes made it clear that he appreciated it. But he shut the conversation down, just the same.

Scarlett nodded. She wanted to think about his reaction, what it could mean, but he gestured for their bill and then there was that to settle.

They were on the road again in minutes and he talked about the pros and cons of paying more for local produce, and did it with enough commitment and interest that Scarlett had to throw herself into the conversation with him.

Really, he was only being sensible, doing what Scarlett should have done from the outset today. He was trying to keep them on a business footing.

So why did Scarlett feel that with each moment that passed the tension and consciousness between them, rather than lessening, became stronger until everything between them seemed to be exaggerated a hundredfold?

She could *hear* each breath he took. The radio was silent. Her own breathing sounded loud to her ears. Each of Lorenzo's words felt like the brush of his hand against her skin. When they fell silent, Scarlett remembered times in their past that they had shared such silences. Companionable, sweet silences.

If she thought this was only affecting her, maybe she would have had a good chance of squashing it back, but it was in his eyes each time he glanced her way. It was in the clench of his hands around the steering wheel and the tight set of his shoulders as he tried so hard to keep their conversation moving and work-focused.

And safe.

When Lorenzo drew the van to a stop in the parking space at the back of the restaurant, Scarlett turned and gave him a subdued smile.

She was trying. She wanted to be wise. If he could try for that then the least she should do was meet him halfway.

Anything else was sheer madness anyway, even if her mind all but refused to consider this fact right now. 'Thank you for the trip, and for letting me bounce all my thoughts off you. That was really helpful.'

Scarlett was proud. The words were coming out and making sense. Later she would be able to really and truly examine all the things they'd talked about. For now she said, 'There are clearly some things I still need to address.'

In fact, she could even think of one of those things right now. 'I need to speak with Luca about these issues with purchasing local goods. What happened with the olives in the end, by the way?'

And see? A sensible, interested question to arm herself with knowledge about that issue, too.

'The grower replaced them with a decent grade and got a warning not to pull a stunt like that again.' Lorenzo stepped from the van and, again, came around it to open her door for her.

His words were clear and to the point and if she hadn't looked into his eyes Scarlett might have believed they could just be friends.

'Good. The grower had better do the right thing next time.' Lorenzo would see that he did. Scarlett felt quite confident of this. Confident enough that she didn't feel the need to manage the situation herself. 'I'm learning to trust you again.' She uttered the words without forethought.

Perhaps they surprised him enough that he didn't think to step out of her path.

Because Scarlett stepped down from the van and all but into his arms. They ended up practically chest-to-chest there in the rear area behind the restaurant. It was quiet and still out here, the van parked close to the back of the building. They stood between the van and a windowless section of wall.

She looked up into his eyes and he looked down into hers and…that was the end of it. The end of days of working with each other and suppressing all sorts of things and today not managing to suppress them.

Scarlett didn't know who kissed whom. She didn't know who made that first infinitesimal move or whether they both did.

All she knew was their lips pressed together in the seclusion of the back area. Lorenzo made a soft sound in the back of his throat.

Their hands rose and arms locked around each other. This wasn't a one-second press of lips against lips and a hurried and startled breaking away. This was the rest of that first kiss. The completion of that first kiss. A giving and taking and offering and receiving that seemed to touch on so much more than a shared attraction or a past closeness.

Scarlett kissed Lorenzo and completely forgot where she was. She forgot her position as Financial Manager of Rosa, forgot that potentially someone could happen along out here. She forget everything except the taste and the touch of him as they held each other close and he kissed her as though he had starved for the taste of her, had needed this intimacy with her. *Had to have it for the sake of his soul.*

Oh, these were dangerous thoughts for Scarlett to have. Dangerous, wanting-to-leap-to-conclusions-that-she-shouldn't-leap-to thoughts. They dissipated anyway into pure sensation before Scarlett could do more than feel the drift of them through the recesses of her mind. Her hand rose and her fingers cupped the nape of his neck. Strong muscle shifted beneath her fingertips as she stroked them softly over his warm skin.

Lorenzo's hands firmed at her waist and their kiss deepened, became an expression of urgency and need that felt more immediate and necessary than ever before.

'I have missed your taste, the touch of you, the scent of you.' He murmured the words as he pressed kisses to the column of her neck, the side of her jaw and across her cheek. Finally, before his mouth closed over hers, he added, 'I have missed *you*, Scarlett. More than I understood. More than I understand now.'

'Lorenzo.' His words were beautiful to her ears and Scarlett gave herself up to kissing him, to the belief in his need for her. She gave and gave and Lorenzo gave back to her, worshipping her mouth with his lips, gently caressing her arms and back and shoulders until she wanted to stay in his arms and never leave.

Would Scarlett have *ever* thought to stop that kiss?

It wasn't a question she could answer because a sound nearby broke them apart like...guilty lovers. In that first moment, Scarlett realised it was only a bird rustling through the branches of a tall bush at the edge of the area.

And then her mind began to function again and she became truly aware once more of their surroundings. She'd kissed Rosa's head chef in plain view of anyone who might have happened out the back door of the premises. She'd kissed Lorenzo and Lorenzo had kissed her right back, as though all of their past hadn't happened and she hadn't been forced to navigate her way through the pain of him totally betraying her back then.

What on *earth* had she been thinking?

'I—I need to work on the books.' Scarlett uttered the words

without any real idea of what she was doing or saying. She needed to escape. That was all she knew.

From what had just happened, from dealing with how it had made her feel, from addressing the issue of…this, whatever 'this' was, altogether.

She didn't wait for him to argue the point or question her or anything else. Something told her he wouldn't have. That he felt just as surprised and taken aback by their actions as she did. They were actions they might have taken five years ago when stealing kisses and being together had felt so exciting to her. And then she'd had to deal with his revelation that he was married, his explanations about the broken state of that marriage.

His promise to make all things right in his world so he and Scarlett…

Not now. You're not thinking about that now.

Scarlett glanced every which way about her to ensure as best she now could, after the fact, that they had indeed *not* been observed in that compromising few moments, and she hurried into the restaurant by the rear door and shut herself in Luca's office, where she proceeded to bury her head in bookwork.

Deeply!

To the point where she had no space to think about anything else whatsoever!

And can you continue to ignore all your thoughts and hope that will be a true answer to anything, Scarlett?

To not only the issue of Lorenzo, but of family, too? Do you want to be close to them, or don't you?

Yes, she did, and Scarlett was trying. These things took time!

CHAPTER SIX

'OH, NO!' Scarlett stared at the e-mail she'd just dug out of the spam folder in her Internet mail program. 'How could this have ended up in the mail trash? What date was it sent? Why didn't they contact me when I didn't respond? What if I've missed out on the opportunity?' As these questions popped out another question followed. She opened the e-mail and started to scan its contents. *'What date* have they said they want to do this?'

It was Friday evening. She'd been just about to pack up in Luca's office and to be honest she had felt a true sense of achievement.

She still didn't have all the answers for making the restaurant completely self-supporting and guaranteed to always run in the black, but the changes she'd made were starting to pay off and she wasn't at the end of her stream of ideas by any means.

This was only the beginning of what Scarlett could do. One of the things she'd tried was to canvas the local promotional body for Monta Correnti to see if she could interest them in granting publicity and media coverage to Rosa for a weekend cook-up. The body had a budget for community-related events, and Scarlett had hoped she might be able to interest them.

Scarlett had logged onto her e-mail account at the last moment just now to check for a response. Because she'd asked about it and time had passed with no answer, she'd all but given up on the possibility. But she had found her answer, sent almost a week ago and hiding out in the mail program's trash file!

She quickly skimmed the contents of the e-mail. The promotional group not only loved the idea she'd put to them, they'd taken it further and brought in a second restaurant so the two could run a 'friendly' cook-off contest. 'Oh, please tell me it's not—'

Sorella.

But of course it was, because they were side by side in the square. The local co-ordinators couldn't imagine anything more exciting or convenient. They anticipated a high degree of interest, advertising would commence… Scarlett read the date and her eyes widened. Advertising would commence *today*. And the contest itself would run *next weekend* with *TV and newspaper coverage*!

'That's only seven days away.' A lump of panic lodged itself in Scarlett's throat, and doubled in size when the remaining implications made themselves felt. 'And they've set us up to compete against Sorella.'

According to this e-mail, Sorella's owner had been more than delighted to front up for a contest to see which restaurant could prepare the best dishes and be declared better than the other.

Oh, Scarlett, what have you got Rosa into? And the family into by letting this come about?

Scarlett's mother would thrive on this kind of competition. It didn't surprise Scarlett that Lisa had agreed to the contest. That was enough of a problem. Scarlett could imagine Lisa hustling her restaurant staff by remote control over the phone from wherever she happened to be at the time, to ensure they did a good job in the contest. If Lisa didn't have other more important engagements, she might even turn up for some part of the weekend.

Unfortunately, Luca might be a little more enthused about the possibility of 'beating' Sorella in a cook-off than anyone in the family would want as well.

Isabella, Jackie, Lizzie and some of the others had all been trying to get things on a better, less confrontational footing between the various branches of the family and specifically between Lisa and Luca.

More rivalry was the last thing they needed and yet now Scarlett had single-handedly set the family up for a cook-off war.

Scarlett dropped her head into her hands where she sat at the desk. 'I can see it now. Front-page news. *Rabble-raising Restaurants in Fantastic Food Fight*. There's no way this can work out well. Either one restaurant loses the challenge or the other one does.'

'If you have a moment.' The words came from the office doorway.

They were tight, low, spoken in a very familiar male voice and they held a decided edge of 'unimpressed' about them. The words were Lorenzo's, but they didn't come from the relaxed, helpful Lorenzo she'd worked with in recent days.

Days in which they'd almost felt as though they were in some kind of holding pattern to Scarlett. They'd kissed beside the van after parking it behind the restaurant. Scarlett had melted into his arms and he'd seemed to need their kiss as much as she had. Since then she hadn't been able to get those moments out of her mind. But nor had she been able to draw any conclusions about them, decide what she should do about them.

In fact, Scarlett had asked herself whether there might be some way that she and Lorenzo could, perhaps, pursue these feelings now.

The thought wasn't an easy one for her to have. He'd broken her heart five years ago. Scarlett had never expected to feel anything again for him other than contempt and anger. But working with him here at Rosa had changed that. They'd developed a mutual respect for each other. Scarlett might have wanted… If Lorenzo had seemed to want to pursue…

Well, so far he's done a good job of not pursuing anything. Maybe he's forgotten all about the kiss. Maybe he kisses women like that all the time.

And maybe her head chef was a little upset right now and Scarlett had better deal with that. He stepped into the office and slapped down a copy of today's newspaper.

One brief glance showed her the feature piece.

Restaurants will break out their competitive spirits for a weekend cook-off next weekend!

'Um, about that.' She really could have done with a few minutes to try to figure out how to present this to him in the best light, now that there was nothing she could do to change the course of events.

It was the end of the day. Why couldn't she have discovered this earlier? Had Lorenzo known about it earlier? 'When did you find out?'

'Just now. None of us had time to look at the paper today.' His gaze held an accusing edge. 'I don't know whether to say it's just as well a patron didn't tell one of us earlier in the day, or wish that they had. At least there'd have been a *bit* more notice.'

Scarlett forced a smile to her face and hoped it was a placatory, calm, very professional one. 'Would you mind if I took a look? I didn't know this was going to be in today's edition of the paper so I haven't actually seen it yet.'

That sounded suitably under control and not totally panic-stricken. Didn't it?

Lorenzo silently pushed the newspaper her way with the

tip of one finger. He still looked ready to pitch a fit over the topic. She should feel defensive about that. No, she should be *aggressive* about it, in an 'I'm in charge here and this is just another aspect of performing your tasks for the restaurant so don't bother complaining about it' kind of a way.

Instead, she kept thinking how strong and manly he looked with his muscles locked that way and irritation and displeasure stamped on his face.

'Right, well, let me just take a quick look.' Scarlett had never skimmed a piece of print quite so quickly. As she did so she felt Lorenzo glowering down at her. She finally forced her gaze up, to meet stormy brown eyes. 'Um, maybe you'd like to shut the door while we discuss this.'

'Shutting the door isn't going to make a bit of difference, Scarlett.' His words weren't shouted, but they were strong enough that they would carry. 'I'm done here for the night, anyway. If you want to maintain some privacy on the topic of an article that *I hadn't even heard about,* I suggest we take this elsewhere.'

Right. Well, that seemed like an eminently sensible idea. Scarlett shot to her feet. That was, *she rose gracefully,* and calmly gathered her laptop into the all-purpose carry bag that housed her room key and other necessary items a girl couldn't do without, and stepped confidently towards the door.

And through it.

Without revealing even slightly that her heart was racing in a highly unprofessional way.

Oh, she wasn't scared of him.

She just hadn't had time to absorb the implications of this arrangement, and therefore didn't exactly have a plan in mind for dealing with Lorenzo's feelings about the whole matter. And she had this compulsive and extremely unprofessional urge to offer to rub his shoulders or in some other way un-ruffle his clearly ruffled feathers for him.

'We'll go to my bedsit. It's close and the owner is away so I know we'll be quite private even if you need to express your sentiments…' Loudly? Vociferously? With gusto? Scarlett decided it might be wiser not to finish that sentence.

Instead she strode through the restaurant ahead of Lorenzo, and they walked in silence across the square to her bedsit. She let them in quickly, set her laptop down carefully against the wall inside the door.

Lorenzo drew a deep breath and advanced two steps into the centre of the room.

Which also brought him two steps closer to Scarlett who happened to be standing just shy of that same centre of the room herself.

'Why is this the first I've heard of a cook-off that's to take place between Sorella and Rosa? What do you hope to achieve from this? Have you thought of the possible ramifications?'

He was unapologetically irritated. And yet his eyes stayed gentle.

Scarlett frowned. Not at Lorenzo, but at her own thoughts. Now was not the time to take stock of Lorenzo's eyes, *or* to feel that she wanted such gentleness from him.

'The response from the local body handling my application ended up in my e-mail spam folder almost a week ago and I didn't find it until today.' Scarlett would contact them to find out just why she'd received no follow-up when she had failed to respond to the e-mail. It really wasn't appropriate for the matter to be settled upon and advertised when one of the restaurants hadn't actually agreed to the terms!

'And don't you think that as Head Chef I might have been made aware that such a cook-off event was a possibility in the first place?' His hands came up to perch on a set of lean hips. 'What if I didn't want to participate in a cook-off?'

'Well—'

'And not only that.' He paced from one end of her very

small living area to the other and back again. 'I've effectively got six days to get ready to do this, and try to make sure that when I participate, Rosa wins. It's not going to look great if we don't, for the restaurant or for my career. I can't afford to lose another job, Scarlett. I'd hoped this job would be different, that I'd have a chance to prove myself and not be judged by rumours spread by Marcel—' He broke off and turned his face away for a moment before he whipped it back. 'This whole thing—'

'Is going to be just fine, despite the fact that I messed up by not following up on my approach to this local body, and by only finding the e-mail in my spam file tonight.' Scarlett owned her mistake without hesitation, and injected all the assurance and confidence into her tone that she could possibly muster.

But in relation to his past jobs, had he been about to speak his ex-wife's name? 'What do you mean—?'

'That's not the point now. Not relevant.' He chopped a hand through the air. 'How long have the Sorella staff known about this event?'

'I'm guessing, from before the date of that e-mail.' Scarlett still wanted to know what Lorenzo had been about to say. Why would Marcella still have anything to say about him after so long?

'So at the least, the Sorella staff have known about this for a week longer than we have.'

Scarlett tried for a conciliatory nod. 'Well, yes, I'm guessing so. This truly wasn't intended as a sleight to you, Lorenzo. I meant to mention the possibility when I first sent the feeler out. In the flurry of other things, I admit I forgot to follow up on that. To complicate matters, I didn't expect to be informed by merely an e-mail that I almost didn't see at all.'

'All right.' He sucked in a deep breath and slowly blew it

out again. 'Things happen. And knowing it wasn't a deliberate decision on your part to not discuss it makes a difference.'

'Thank you.' Scarlett acknowledged the level of her relief wasn't only in relation to keeping him happy in terms of work. She didn't want Lorenzo to be upset with her. Period.

Oh, Scarlett. Don't start to need his approval or need him too much. You mustn't let your emotions get involved with him a second time.

Well, of course she wouldn't do that. Certainly she wouldn't fall in love with him again or something equally silly. But liking. Liking him was okay.

Wasn't it? 'The approach that I made was actually for Rosa to do a weekend cooking demonstration by ourselves, but somebody has apparently decided it would be more interesting and exciting if we cooked against another restaurant. And they chose Sorella. I didn't look for either of those things to happen, and I didn't anticipate not being given a chance to turn the idea down rather than my agreement on behalf of Rosa being assumed the way it has been.'

'But if you turn around now and refuse to participate, Rosa will look bad.' He nodded his head. 'Well, that means the choice is made. I've seen events similar to this on television.' He frowned. 'Not entirely similar, I suppose, but I can understand how the body would have thought a cook-off between two restaurants would be more exciting than a sole performance.'

Scarlett nodded. 'And with the two restaurants side by side, diners will be able to observe the goings-on from their tables. I'm guessing the judging will take place outside in the square, between the two restaurants. 'In fact, it will make a fabulous outside event,' Scarlett murmured as the possibilities began to register. Yes, she could see pitfalls, too many of them, but she was also starting to see real potential.

Excitement started to bubble and she hurried on. 'You're

so good at what you do, 'Renz. I didn't get to see the full end results of that special lunch you prepared the first day, but you proved that day that you can work under pressure. I've seen everything that's come out of the kitchen since, and tasted a variety of the meals you prepare on a regular basis. The one thing I'm not worried about is what you can do with food to give Sorella a run for their money in a contest.'

She stepped past him to retrieve her laptop, opened it and set it on the small kitchenette bench top. 'Let's read the e-mail through properly. I may have missed something the first time. The newspaper article…?'

'Is right here.' He picked up the newspaper from her sofa where he'd dropped it, and for the first time seemed to actually look around him.

At a small room, with the two of them inside it and, aside from the tiny table and chairs, the only piece of furniture was the sofa that was her lounging area by day, and her bed by night.

Suddenly *Scarlett* felt a little too aware of this confined space, and their isolation together within it.

Not going there, Scarlett.

'The, uh, the newspaper article says that the two restaurants will be cooking against each other in…' Lorenzo bent his head and seemed to force his attention to the printed words '…"A spell-binding weekend of fabulous food, speed-cooking, and excitement galore. Table bookings commence as of Monday. Don't miss out, this is going to be amazing."'

'It's good advertising.' Scarlett had leaned in to read along with him.

Not because she wanted an excuse to be closer to him. She proved this by stepping quite calmly away and moving the two steps to the kitchenette bench and bringing the laptop out of sleep mode. Since it hadn't been shut down, the e-mail appeared on the screen straight away and Scarlett read it with complete attention.

Silently.

While Lorenzo also read silently over *her* shoulder.

So close that she could turn her head just the tiniest bit and their lips could meet.

'It—the e-mail says right here…' She pointed at the screen, as though that would help anything.

Well, it helped her to force her attention to that screen. Somewhat. If she didn't count the portion of her interest that refused to step away, metaphorically or otherwise, from Lorenzo's nearness.

He radiated consciousness of her in the same way she was radiating consciousness of him. '*The e-mail says* that the restaurants will compete in several events over the weekend, starting on Friday night, and that for one event at least each restaurant will cook to its strengths using established meals from its regular menu.'

'So authentic Italian for us, and international cuisine for Sorella. That gives them a lot broader range.' His breath brushed across her cheek as he spoke.

'Which gives them more to work with to make mistakes, choose dishes the judges may not approve of, and to second-guess themselves on what's going to be the best for the contest.' Scarlett turned her head, met his gaze, acknowledged how close they stood to each other and how far this had now gone from their initial discussion when she'd been concerned about smoothing his ruffled feathers.

'Rosa may have a less diverse menu, but every item on it is authentic cuisine for this region and for Italy. I'm seeing that as a good thing for us.' She hoped her words made sense; that they came across as focused and alert. Because a part of her could only focus on him.

How had they progressed to this point with each other in

what was really a short space of time since they met again? How had *she* progressed? From the bitterness of the way he had hurt her, to a part of her wanting to…go back to that place with him again?

If that happened, it would be different this time. Lorenzo was a free agent. Yet he'd mentioned Marcella as though she had some kind of ongoing impact in his life. When had he left his wife? How long had they been divorced? Had it been very acrimonious? Was that why Lorenzo didn't seem to want to speak about it, and perhaps why Marcella was a little bitter or something?

Well, of course his ex-wife would be bitter.

And Scarlett was *not* seriously considering a rematch with Lorenzo. That would be a hundred times worse than a restaurant war, and more dangerous to her emotional health.

'It *is* a good plan, Scarlett.' He said it with commitment. 'If it's handled right, maybe we can use it to our advantage.'

'Can you prepare adequately in the time frame? What can I do to help you get ready for the event, and to handle it next weekend?' She *had* to force her thoughts and focus onto these things. 'If you need time off before then, consultation about menu choices, extra shopping done for you?'

'I'll need an extra kitchen hand for the entire weekend. At least one.' He watched as she shut down the laptop and, without thinking about it, Scarlett led the way to the sofa, sat, and gestured for him to do likewise, which he did.

The thing dipped in the middle. Like one of those love seats made especially for cuddling. Made so you couldn't *avoid* cuddling. She hadn't actually sat on it with another person since she rented the bedsit.

Scarlett's face heated as her hip brushed against his. She moved a little away, but their bodies still leaned in towards each other. 'I'll find you a kitchen hand.'

'They'll need to be willing to take orders, and to know

enough about Italian cooking to not need to be instructed over every little thing.' His fingers shifted over the fabric of the sofa cushion. 'Cooking on a deadline, I'll want every hand available and even that may not be enough. Not if we're catering meals for patrons at the same time.'

'I'll make sure you have what you need, Lorenzo.' Scarlett made him the assurance, and then became lost in eyes that silently let her know there were other needs. Needs that matched hers. For touch. For the brush of skin against skin that could turn the simple stroke of fingers over the back of a hand from simplicity to desire.

What did he want of her? Really? What did Scarlett want of him? What was there about Marcella? 'Please, will you tell me about the past?'

'I must go.' He got to his feet and strode to the door.

She'd uttered her words softly, and he'd spoken at the same time. Scarlett didn't know if he'd heard her request and probably it was better if he hadn't. To start digging around in that now...

But there were things she wanted to know. Maybe she could ask Isabella without making it appear that she was particularly interested for her own sake.

Scarlett followed Lorenzo to the door. 'I'm glad we were able to discuss this calmly and work things out, and I do apologise for the way it all ended up coming about.'

'I'm sorry I let myself make assumptions before you'd had a chance to explain what happened.' He turned the knob and opened the door, and glanced back at her over his shoulder. 'I'll give you a menu list tomorrow morning so you can think about the costs that will be involved.'

'Yes.' She nodded her head. 'We'll get full into planning first thing tomorrow. At Rosa.'

As opposed to here.

Because *here,* with its closeness and privacy, was not a

good idea for them. They needed to concentrate on their work, didn't they? Lorenzo seemed very determined to do that, and only that. In fact since the moment he'd half mentioned his ex-wife, his attitude had seemed to focus on getting out of here, getting things back to a working footing.

'Goodbye, Scarlett. We'll speak tomorrow.' He stepped through her door, closed it after himself, and disappeared.

And Scarlett told herself to be very pleased with the outcome of this meeting. They'd discussed the necessary issues, kept it away from the other staff at Rosa while they sorted out their differences about the upcoming event.

They were in accord now. They would be able to not only cope with the cook-off, but she was certain Lorenzo would do a great job and she would make sure he had the support staff around him to make success as easy as possible for him to achieve.

Overall, it was a great outcome.

Even if he hadn't kissed her.

Particularly because he didn't kiss you, Scarlett. Being kissed by the man who broke your heart and let you down five years ago is the last thing you want!

He *had* let her down.

But Scarlett was beginning to think about the fact that she hadn't exactly been without blame in that situation, either. She'd expected him to leave his wife for her. What if she hadn't understood how difficult that might have been for him at that time? Maybe there'd been reasons?

Oh. She couldn't believe she was thinking that!

With a shake of her head, Scarlett pushed the thoughts aside and went back to her laptop. If she and Lorenzo were to make a success of this cook-off and do it well for Rosa, she'd better get cracking to figure out how to ensure he had enough staff and everything else he would need. *Those* were appropriate thoughts.

She took her mobile phone from her pocket and phoned the restaurant to speak to Isabella. Her cousin was busy in the kitchen so the conversation was brief, though Scarlett promised to fill her in about upcoming events first thing tomorrow. 'Come here for a coffee, Izzie.'

If Scarlett also hoped to grill Izzie about Lorenzo's past, well, a good financial manager *needed* to understand where her staff were coming from so she could best deal with them.

Right. Sure. That was what it was all about.

Scarlett thought about Luca and Lisa and their long-standing rivalry, and where this cook-off could put everyone in the family.

She had better figure out how to discuss *this news* with the family at large, and quickly, and hope they didn't feel she'd thrown Lisa and Luca at each other's throats.

Because that wouldn't exactly look like an attempt at helping the two to get along better!

CHAPTER SEVEN

SCARLETT stood to the side of the courtyard dining area of Rosa the following Friday and asked herself where the time had gone between her decision to grill Isabella about Lorenzo's past, and now.

The cook-off was about to start. Lorenzo had worked so hard all week, preparing for it, thinking about dishes, working things out. Scarlett had worked equally hard to get him the extra workers he'd need, to get as much advertising out as she could to augment what was already out there and yet without costing Rosa too much in doing that. The focus was to bring diners in for the event, because diners meant money, and money helped Rosa's bottom line. They couldn't really afford for this weekend to run at a loss.

'Visitors, diners and friends, what you are seeing here tonight is the beginning of a very exciting Monta Correnti event.' The head of the local entertainment body spoke into her microphone with just the right edge of dramatic effect to ensure she had the attention of everyone in the square.

Every seat, indoor and outdoor, at both Sorella and Rosa was taken. That side of the hard work *had* paid off.

Lorenzo had been focused and really supportive about the event. He might not have been impressed with the short notice at first, but once the idea was on the table, he had got one hundred percent behind it.

His attitude, well, it made Scarlett proud. And then, of course, there'd been dealing with the family. It hadn't been easy to try to convince everyone that first of all she'd meant no harm, secondly the die was cast, and thirdly if they all tried to get along this could still be okay.

'I hope this event turns out to be worth the trouble, Scarlett.' Her mother's words sounded behind her. 'Since I've flown in especially for it.'

Scarlett dragged her gaze from where Lorenzo was setting up his outdoor workstation. She hadn't even realised she'd been watching him with avid eyes. Hopefully no one else had noticed that. There literally hadn't been a moment of privacy between Scarlett and Lorenzo all week. Not one where they'd been alone for any length of time, had any opportunity...

To what? Talk? Catch up on old news? Kiss each other silly? Did Lorenzo even really want that any more? Maybe he'd decided that them mixing business and personal issues, at all in any shape or form, was a really bad idea.

Which of course was exactly what Scarlett herself should have decided long before now, and *had* decided before she came to Monta Correnti. She just hadn't managed to hold on very well to that conviction. Scarlett didn't know what to do about that, and...her emotions were a little raw anyway from dealing with a week of trying to smooth tensions within the family while simultaneously trying to be as supportive as possible to Rosa's head chef as he prepared for this weekend.

And while carrying on with the necessary work of studying how Rosa ticked in every way conceivable, studying the various staff members. Scarlett had her doubts about the suitability of a couple of them, though at least the woman whose shift had been pulled forward by an hour appeared to have accepted the change and knuckled back down to concentrating on her work.

Well, now there was Mamma to deal with.

And Uncle Luca standing over there, glaring in Mamma's direction. Scarlett pushed back a sigh.

'Mum. It's nice to see you.' *Sort of.* 'Actually, the cook-off developed out of quite a different idea. It wasn't initially intended to be anything more than—'

'A chance for you to try to convince the world that Rosa is up to Sorella's standards of excellence and can provide the same kind of international cuisine?' Lisa shook her head. 'Oh, I heard about your chef stealing the show with that meal he cooked for the movie star.'

'Rosa was approached to do that work. Nothing more.' Scarlett stopped before anything more could be said on that topic. She wasn't about to bring on an argument with her mother. 'I'd like to hope this cook-off can be a positive thing for both Sorella and Rosa.' Scarlett chose her words carefully. She didn't address her mother's assumption that Rosa was about to start trying to cook international cuisine.

It might be silly, but what if Rosa one day did want to add some international dishes to its menu? Scarlett didn't want to rule out that possibility in discussion with her mother. 'Both restaurants can really benefit from this weekend. I hope you'll look at the cook-off in that light. Not so much as a contest, but as a means for both restaurants to display their strengths.'

'Well, I guess we'll see what transpires. Excuse me for a moment, Scarlett. I want to touch base with my chef before the contest actually starts.' Lisa walked away and spoke for a few moments with her head chef.

As she did so the camera panned across the square. The woman at the microphone explained the outdoor cooking set-up—provided by Sorella because their chef had a relative able to get access to the equipment cheaply.

In fact, the local body and the two restaurants had managed an excellent level of co-operation when it came to the nuts and bolts organisation of the event. Because of those cameras, Scarlett pinned on a professional smile.

In fact, when she glanced at her mother she saw some of her own expression reflected on her face.

Scarlett wasn't entirely like Lisa. But there were parts of her mother in her, and sometimes their minds worked similarly.

With that in mind, when Lisa returned to stand at her side Scarlett tried to sell the idea to her mother in a way Lisa could, hopefully, respect. 'This event has already shown that the staff of the two restaurants can co-operate to reach a common goal, and the event itself has increased business for Sorella *and* Rosa.

'We're getting some free media advertising out of it. You didn't have to come back for the event, but now that you have I hope you can at least see that this is a good thing.'

'Good in some ways perhaps.' Lisa's gaze moved to the front of Rosa where Luca stood. She murmured, 'Of course, Sorella will win the contest.'

'You and Uncle Luca—' Scarlett bit her lip before she faced her mother squarely. 'No one in the family wants this to turn into anything unpleasant. The purpose of the weekend is to promote *both* restaurants. Please promise me you won't start any conflict with Uncle Luca about it.'

'I have no desire to fight with your uncle.' Lisa's words were a little sharp. After that she excused herself with a brief nod and returned to Sorella.

Scarlett noted the fact that she had been given an assurance of sorts, but not a complete promise. She pushed back a sigh and her gaze returned to Lorenzo. Almost as though he sensed her unease, he looked up and caught her glance on him.

Even from this distance Scarlett saw his eyes soften and the slightest hint of a smile touch the corners of his mouth before he checked everything one last time and stood waiting at his workstation.

Izzie had cancelled coffee the other morning, and Scarlett hadn't got her opportunity to ask her questions. There hadn't been time since. But that look just now hadn't seemed uninterested.

'Gentleman chefs, are you ready?' The MC glanced at each of them. 'Everyone, please focus your attention on the time because this amazing cooking marathon will start in five, four, three, two…'

The countdown ended with a cheer from the dining crowd. Lorenzo and the other chef glanced at each other and got to work. Scarlett watched with her heart in her throat. Her level of nerves was ridiculous, and she wasn't even the one up there.

Oh, but she wanted Lorenzo to succeed. For Rosa, yes, but most of all because he was an excellent chef and Scarlett realised she wanted to see his talent recognised. The other chef was efficient and moved quickly. For tonight they had a low-range budget, two hours only to prepare and plate their dishes, and they were preparing one meal and two side dishes from their restaurant's existing menus.

Oh, Scarlett wanted to be up there at Lorenzo's side, cheering him on. She had to get her nervous energy under control or she'd be a wreck before the night was over!

For a moment Scarlett wished she could follow in Isabella's footsteps for the night, and hide out in Rosa's inside kitchen. But Isabella was needed there to supervise the production of those meals while Lorenzo was otherwise occupied. Scarlett's job was to pitch in anywhere if she saw a need, but mostly to be Rosa's representative to media and anyone else interested for the evening.

Scarlett tore her gaze from Lorenzo's efficient and appealing workmanship. Truly, she couldn't see how he would do other than come out as a favourite in terms of how much the media would like him. Not that this was a man-judging contest, of course. It was a *food-judging* contest. Totally and utterly, and Lorenzo's good looks had nothing to do with it.

Where was she?

Oh, yes. Scarlett forced herself to step through the crowd and start hustling for Rosa. There were people here tonight, diners who didn't come here often, and people from out of town, and others of note whom Scarlett should meet and greet.

It was Scarlett's job to help them appreciate the beauty of Rosa so they would come back soon, bring their families and friends, tell their co-workers. Tonight was about food and contest and media attention, but it was also about word-of-mouthing a commodity so more people would try it, and come back to it again and again.

Scarlett kept Lorenzo in the corner of her eye while she went about winning over Rosa's diners.

'You're frowning, little sister.' Jackie's voice sounded beside Scarlett.

It was one hour and fifty-three minutes later, not that Scarlett had been counting or compulsively checking her watch.

There was no need now. Their MC for the evening had commenced a verbal countdown for the final ten minutes and was asking questions of Lorenzo and the other chef as they put the finishing touches to their dishes and prepared to serve them.

The crowd was enthralled. Everyone wanted to know which dishes would be the winners. The whole event was on show on large screens erected inside and outside both restaurants so that all the diners could see.

'I've asked a lot of Lorenzo.' Scarlett uttered the words to Jackie.

Scarlett *had* settled down somewhat from her earlier state

of feeling totally nerve-racked. But those nerves were back and fluttering about inside her again now.

For tonight Scarlett had dressed in a plain black sleeveless dress with black pumps on her feet. Her only concession to colour was a cream ribbon in her hair to match the pearl drop earrings and necklace she wore with the dress.

She'd wanted to blend in if she felt like blending, but still look professional. Scarlett's hand rose to the pearl drop necklace. It was a step up from fiddling with her hair ribbon, she supposed. And tonight she *had* used mousse. Enough to keep her hair in place no matter what! 'He looks so calm, but cooking in this kind of environment under the eagle eye of so many diners, let alone the dignitaries who'll do the judging, has to be really stressful.'

Jackie cast a thoughtful glance her way. 'I suppose you'd have spent a considerable amount of time with Lorenzo since you started working at Rosa, but you sound almost—'

Half in love with him? Overprotective? Too interested? 'Stressed? Yes. Yes, I have been. It's been a big week.'

Scarlett would have blabbed on further, but her sister didn't let her.

Instead she gave Scarlett a very direct look. 'I hope you aren't falling for him or anything, Scarlett. He keeps to himself, but you do know—'

'And we're into the final few seconds now, people, so let's count them down.' The MC began a backwards count, and whatever else Jackie might have planned to say gave way to the surge of excitement through the crowd as they counted down the final seconds of the two-hour block of time.

Scarlett felt she had been saved by the bell. She had to be more careful about what showed on her face. It would be mortifying for people to start to see that...

What? That she was half in love with Lorenzo again?

Not that. Of course not that. But...attracted to him. She

didn't want people to notice that she was attracted to him. Work needed to be work and only that. Business and personal, those two things shouldn't be mixed.

Maybe she should have thought of that before kissing him so thoroughly that day. It was only luck that they hadn't been seen at that time.

The other chef fussed until the final second, straightening a garnish on one of the plates while Lorenzo checked his meal one last time for standard of presentation. They stood back as the MC called, 'Time is up.'

Most of the diners were at the coffee stage of their meals now. The staff had done a good job of looking after everyone. Isabella had clearly done a good job supervising in the kitchen, because Scarlett had been receiving compliments on Rosa's cuisine all night.

No doubt the same had occurred for her mother as she strolled between tables at Sorella, stopping at this one and then that to offer a few words. Lisa did this well. Scarlett also did this well. Not that she was being competitive in thinking such a thing.

As the judges took their seats to taste the meals, Scarlett turned to Jackie. 'Will you excuse me?' Her gaze returned to Lorenzo. 'I need—'

To be there with Lorenzo while this round is decided.

Not because she felt the need to offer the man emotional support. Certainly not because she felt the need for some herself, right now. Scarlett glanced again at her mother, and Luca, who were at this moment casting quite open challenging stares towards each other. 'I need to position myself to handle it if our mother and our uncle decide to blow up when the winner is announced.'

Most of all Scarlett wanted to be at Lorenzo's side, because if they didn't win she didn't want him to feel as though he hadn't made a great achievement for the evening.

'I'll go and get ready to speak with Mum.' Jackie made this announcement with a determined glint in her eye. 'If nothing else, I may be able to distract her from having words with Luca, depending on the outcome of this round. We all want peace within the family. I'm not prepared to let Mum and Luca mess that up at this event.'

'Thanks, Jackie.' Scarlett made her way towards Lorenzo. As she approached the dais he gestured with his hand.

It was the slightest thing, but it showed he wanted her company, and for some ridiculous reason this made Scarlett feel...wonderful.

'The meals and side dishes were all of excellent standard.' One of the judges had taken the microphone and now complimented both Lorenzo and the other chef.

As Scarlett came to Lorenzo's side he dipped his head to whisper quietly, 'From the judges' reactions I think Sorella might have a slight edge over us.'

This *was* the consensus of the judges, and Rosa came in second for this round, though by a very small margin.

'Tomorrow our chefs will cook all day in their kitchens rather than outdoors. You'll be able to watch on the big screens again.' The MC smiled and raised her brows. 'At the end of it, there will be five wonderful desserts prepared for *all* our patrons to taste if they so desire, whether they be guests of Sorella or Rosa. So do come back and have another wonderful meal, and cap it off with a fabulous dessert of your choice!'

A round of applause followed.

Lorenzo waited to speak until the applause had finished. He turned then and congratulated the Sorella chef and they exchanged a few words about the evening before Lorenzo turned back to Scarlett. 'I need to get cleared up here, now that the pressure is off.'

'What you need to do is eat and rest for a while and regain your strength after that marathon effort.' Scarlett said it rather bossily, and yes, she was the boss, but that wasn't the point. 'That is, I mean to say that you must be tired. I know it's been a draining night for me, and I was only worrying about how you would do and whether you'd be okay with it if your dishes didn't win.'

And Scarlett had worried whether they would make a profit for the night, and whether Lisa and Luca would get in a fight.

Scarlett glanced about them. She'd completely forgotten her mother and uncle in the past few minutes. She hadn't even looked to see how either of them had reacted to the results. So much for positioning herself!

'Oh, damn—drat—*dash it all.*' Lisa and Luca were discussing the outcome, all right. With the media. 'Lorenzo…'

'Shall we go together?' He used his hand to give her a gentle push in that direction. A few moments later they were at Luca and Lisa's sides.

The Sorella chef joined them.

Sorella staff members efficiently cleared away after their chef. Scarlett wished she'd thought to ask Rosa's staff to do the same. She glanced over her shoulder and discovered Jackie supervising exactly that. Her sister didn't normally work at Rosa, but she and Romano had both helped out tonight. They'd spent the evening replenishing supplies of wines and topping up carafes of water, clearing dishes and generally helping however they could.

Scarlett drew a deep breath and pasted on a smile, and waded straight up to her uncle and mother. She kissed both of them on each cheek. 'Tonight has been wonderfully successful and fun for both restaurants.'

The interviewer murmured agreement and asked Lorenzo and Sorella's head chef how it felt to cook on a time crunch like that, using different equipment and with a live audience watching their every move.

Lorenzo and the Sorella chef opened up, discussing the challenges of the evening and both agreeing that they wouldn't mind a meal now and a soothing glass of wine. But neither of them wanted to eat the meals they had just cooked. Something else would be nice, preferably cooked by *someone* else!

Everyone laughed and their interviewer wrapped things up, thanked them for their time and moved off. That left five people standing about, and the Sorella chef quickly excused himself. 'It's an early start tomorrow and a big day. I want to check on things in my kitchen and then get some sleep.'

'Lorenzo, you should also get your rest.' Did Scarlett sound like a training coach? Or…a little too possessive of him?

For some inexplicable reason, there under the watchful eyes of her uncle and mother, Scarlett felt suddenly guilty and felt warmth amass at the base of her neck and try very hard to climb into her cheeks.

Scarlett forced the blush back and rubbed her hands together. 'Well, it was a fabulous night. Mum, are you staying for the full weekend or heading off first thing in the morning?' Scarlett would be happy to see her mother to the airport herself. She didn't mean that unkindly, but with Luca and Lisa both present the potential for an explosion was definitely greater.

'If you were staying at my villa,' Lisa said, 'you'd know the answer to that already.'

'Um, well, yes, perhaps that's true.' Scarlett didn't want to address that topic. They'd covered the ground already.

'I'm staying,' Lisa declared. 'This is my restaurant, after all.'

And oddly enough, when Scarlett glanced at her uncle he seemed to be quite pleased by this news. In a real, genuine way rather than a competitive one? Luca turned away a moment later with some muttered comment about speaking with Isabella before he left for the night.

A Sorella guest approached Lisa and wanted to introduce her to his dining companion, and Lisa, too, disappeared.

Scarlett's hand rose to the back of her head. She resisted the urge to tug on her ponytail and dropped her hand back to her side. 'Come back to the kitchen, Lorenzo. They'll still be working in there, but only on clean-up.'

In the time the media interview had taken place, all but a couple of guests had cleared from Rosa's dining tables. 'We'll get some food. We can eat in Luca's office.'

Her uncle was already on his way out of the kitchen as they stepped inside it.

Isabella glanced up and gave a quick smile. 'That was a good effort tonight, Lorenzo. I kept meals for you and Scarlett. We're clearing things away here now. The kitchen will be pristine for your early start tomorrow. We served a lot of meals tonight, too.'

Her eyes glowed as she turned to Scarlett. 'Between my father and your mother, I was worried about this, but it's definitely been good for business. I'm glad you thought of it.'

'Well, I thought of something a bit different and we sort of landed ourselves in the rest of it whether we felt ready or not.' Scarlett cast a glance towards Lorenzo as she said this. 'I'm fortunate that our head chef can work well under pressure and has been very supportive.'

This was true, and Scarlett wanted and maybe *needed* to say it.

Isabella handed meals to them, and poured them a glass of wine each. 'Go eat.'

They went into Luca's office. Scarlett pulled her chair around and Lorenzo pulled the other one in, and they sat side by side and enjoyed exceptional authentic Italian food.

'Isabella did a great job tonight.' Scarlett offered the words as she took a sip of her wine. With the office door pushed across, not closed but it might as well have been, it felt quiet and isolated and somehow…intimate in here.

Because of that she felt the need to fill the silence with words, and went on. 'You did a great job, too. I still think you should have won.'

He took another bite of the meal before he smiled and answered. 'I didn't see you tasting any of the meals.'

'Well, no, I wasn't on the voting panel.' She shook her head. And then she shook it again. 'You were only teasing me. I must be more exhausted than I think, if I can miss something like that.'

'We're both tired.' His hand lifted to tug gently on her ponytail.

It was the silliest thing but she'd pushed the memory from her mind, of him doing that years ago when they were together. Now she remembered and her feelings melted. Maybe Scarlett *was* really tired because she felt as though her defences were down. Her body froze into place, not wanting to move, not wanting him to lower his hand. Craving contact, craving his touch, his attention.

Oh, Scarlett, what are you thinking?

But Scarlett couldn't really think, because suddenly both Lorenzo's hands were there, and he murmured, 'Your ribbon's half falling out.'

His gaze locked with hers and his fingers gently retied the ribbon. It was just his fingers touching her hair, brushing for a moment against the nape of her neck.

So why did he lean in and she lean in? They came so close to kissing. They were almost there with his hands still lifted to her hair and their bodies close and their mouths moving towards each other until someone called out a goodbye from the kitchen.

Someone else answered and Scarlett remembered they were here at Rosa, and what on earth was she doing? Thinking?

Maybe he remembered, too, because he dropped his hands.

'Tomorrow.' Scarlett half turned from him and her hands busied themselves gathering their dinnerware, needlessly fussing over the task. 'It'll be a big day for you and you'll be working around the staff while they prepare the regular meals.'

'It'll be fine.' He got up and held the door open and Scarlett carried the dinnerware while he carried the wineglasses.

They took it all into the kitchen and got pushed out again firmly and quickly by the few remaining staff, headed up by Isabella.

Scarlett's cousin clicked her tongue and made shooing motions with her hands. 'Go home, both of you.'

So Scarlett and Lorenzo went. There were still plenty of local people milling about outside, saying farewells to each other, discussing the evening.

'I should go, too.' As though Lorenzo had invited her to stand around talking to him. Scarlett cleared her throat. 'Thank you for all that you did for tonight's event. It was a really good start to the contest.'

'I hope I can get a win for Rosa tomorrow.' Lorenzo walked with her a few paces. 'This weekend *is* something that can be of real benefit to the restaurant. I'm glad it came about, Scarlett. Your initial idea was good, and, with the way it has now developed, there's probably even more potential to get Rosa a bit more attention and hopefully ongoing patronage.'

'Yes, it's been an interesting experience so far.' Scarlett's glance roved the area. Guests from Sorella and Rosa mingled in groups, chatting. Here and there Scarlett heard snatches of discussion about the meals. One couple said they'd have liked to try foods from both menus. Scarlett's gaze narrowed and she tipped her head to the side.

When she returned her gaze to Lorenzo he was stifling a yawn.

Scarlett snapped to attention. A weary one admittedly, but attention just the same. 'Thanks again. I'll be here first thing tomorrow morning to support you in any way I can. If tonight's event hits any papers tomorrow I hope the coverage will be positive. Hopefully they'll keep it all in a good light.'

If Lisa and Luca played by those rules, too, the whole weekend might actually achieve a lot of good things. 'The family did all pull together, mostly, to try to make tonight a success.'

'Yes.' Lorenzo glanced towards her temporary home across the square. 'I'll see you home.'

'Oh, no, please, don't worry.' Scarlett gestured around them. 'As you can see, there are still plenty of people about and it's only a skip and a jump. You go home and get some rest. I want my head chef to be bright and well rested in the morning.'

If she placed any particular emphasis on the word 'my' it was purely incidental.

Scarlett turned and forced her feet to take her swiftly away from him.

She had to remember he was exactly that, an employee at Rosa and nothing else to her. Whether he'd kissed her in the back parking area behind the restaurant or not. Whether they'd once been so much more to each other, or not.

It wasn't as though they could wind back time and be together as they had been back then. That whole relationship had turned out to be an utter disaster in the end and Scarlett had got really hurt.

So remember that, Scarlett Gibson, and don't set yourself up to get hurt again.

Scarlett tipped her face up and stuck her chin out at the most in-control-of-herself-and-her-life angle she could manage. She strode purposefully to her bedsit where she proceeded to enter, get ready for bed, and then lie and stare at the ceiling while she didn't think once about Lorenzo or replay every nuance of the evening over and over in her mind, with her emotions swinging this way and that way right along with that mental journey.

Non-existent mental journey, Scarlett corrected silently, and rolled onto her tummy and gave the pillow a whack with her hand before she buried her nose in it.

Sleep.

All she wanted to do was sleep.

When she woke in the morning everything would feel much clearer and she'd be totally focused in all the ways that she needed to be.

Scarlett flipped over and squashed the pillow between her hands. She tried burying her nose in it that way and tried equally hard to force her thoughts to blankness.

They weren't making any sense, just going around and around without ever coming to any conclusions. She couldn't think about the evening without always coming back to Lorenzo. On a personal level.

No, they are not doing that!

Oh, yes, they are!

Scarlett gave up on trying to make the pillow into a slumber-inducing shape, flipped onto her back and stared fixedly through the darkness at where the ceiling was, not that she could see it. By the power of her determination if nothing else, she *would* sleep.

And no, she was *not* avoiding any issues by wanting to do only that. She was being a sensible restaurant manager and family liaison.

Yes. That was how it was!

CHAPTER EIGHT

'WHERE is Rocco? Shouldn't he be here for his shift by now?'
As Lorenzo asked the question Scarlett stepped into the busy kitchen.

A frown formed between her brows and she walked swiftly towards him. She looked neat as a pin today, fresh and lovely in a simple white sleeveless blouse over a tan skirt.

On her feet she wore closed-in shoes with good supportive soles, and Lorenzo had the passing thought that only his Scarlett would be able to don shoes like that and look sexy in them. But of course Scarlett was not 'his' anything, other than his boss here at Rosa. He'd been trying to remember that. Trying not to still want her, desire her, be attracted to her.

It's not only those things. There are emotions involved in this for you, at least to some degree. You should admit it, be honest about it to yourself, anyway.

As he'd been honest with her five years ago? Hiding, at first, the fact that he was married? He'd fallen hard for Scarlett. There'd never been anyone in his life who'd affected him the way she had. Making sensible choices had given way to need and love. And for him, that all had happened at a vulnerable time of his life.

His relationship with his wife had been unspeakable at that time. Emotionally torturous for him because of Marcella's... debasing behaviour. The love had been over, and yet Lorenzo had been trapped. He'd craved an escape that wouldn't come. Marcella had trapped him in that way, too.

He had his share of regrets. Loss of a meaningful relationship with his parents thanks to the difficulties with Marcella had been part of that. He'd only come back to Monta Correnti for the position at Rosa. There wasn't much here for him now where family was concerned. A father who'd told him he had dishonoured the family name by leaving Marcella. Lorenzo's two brothers were a little more understanding, but they didn't live here.

One thing Lorenzo did know. He couldn't become emotionally involved with Scarlett again. He was not in a position to do that.

Scarlett joined him and glanced down at the large bowl he held in one hand as he plied a whisk through the contents with the other. 'Can I talk without distracting you?'

'Yes, it's fine.' And it was fine on two counts. They weren't being filmed right now. The technicians needed short breaks occasionally and were on one now, so they could speak without their words being broadcast to diners.

'You asked about Rocco. I know the rosters for this weekend off by heart. He was due here twenty minutes ago.' Scarlett's glance roved his face as she spoke, lingered on his mouth and quickly snapped back up to his eyes. She drew a rapid breath. 'I thought he must have slipped in and I hadn't noticed his arrival.'

No one seemed to know why the man was absent, but Lorenzo wasn't too surprised. Rocco had skipped more shifts in the last month or so than he should have. He always had a handy excuse, but Lorenzo had warned him twice already to pull up his socks.

'I don't want to judge him, but I can't say I was entirely impressed with Rocco when I first met him.' Scarlett turned back to the door. 'Excuse me. I'll try to phone him from the office now.'

Lorenzo watched her leave. He couldn't afford to feel distracted, but nor could he fail to be, it seemed. He wanted to hug Scarlett and assure her that it didn't matter if the kitchen hand was absent. They would get by. It wasn't ideal to be one short but he knew the rest of the staff would pull together and do well if it was necessary, even a person down.

These protective and co-operative feelings that he experienced towards Scarlett would be fine if they were a married couple running their own small restaurant together. To a degree the feelings were half acceptable in terms of their co-management positions here, anyway.

He just happened to know that, for him, his feelings were now a lot more complicated than those of a fellow-employee with Scarlett. There. He had admitted it.

Complicated but still very manageable, he immediately added.

As he thought this Scarlett returned.

Lorenzo glanced up as he poured the whisked dessert mixture into a setting tray. He covered it and placed it carefully in the refrigerator. 'How did you get on?'

'I can't raise a response by phone.' Her teeth tugged at her lower lip. 'Can you have one of the other hands instruct me to do his chores? Or rearrange things so I take care of chores I can't get wrong, and the others cover his duties between them?'

'You, too, have other duties.' Lorenzo looked into Scarlett's lovely eyes.

And discovered a dose of determination staring back at him.

She stuck her chin out. 'The most important duty is ensuring that my head chef has all the help he needs.'

And the truth was that Lorenzo *was* hard at work on

his dessert preparation. The other staff were hard at work on lunchtime meals for a restaurant floor that was rapidly filling.

It wasn't a good time to be a staff member short, and it wasn't a good time for Lorenzo to be distracted by other aspects of the kitchen. Not if they wanted to win this round of the contest, and trying to do that was important for Rosa, too. 'All right. You can don an apron and get the others to show you what they most need you to do, but only while you're really needed in here.'

'Isabella won't be here until mid-afternoon.' Scarlett bit her lip. 'I could try to get her to come in earlier but I spoke to her on the phone this morning and she said that she and Jackie had invited Mum to have lunch with them. It wasn't really based in…social intentions.'

'A little bit of distraction.' He nodded. 'And we don't want your mother to think we're not coping in here.' That was something Lorenzo could completely understand.

Scarlett nodded. 'If I call Isabella, she and Jackie might both feel obligated to leave their lunch and come in, and that leaves Mum on the loose, um, I mean…'

'You mean *on the loose*.' Lorenzo grinned, a completely spontaneous outright grin as he watched a lovely little rush of colour leach into Scarlett's cheeks. And then his smile faded, because she was so beautiful. All he wanted in that moment was to kiss her. He shut down the response, but he suspected it would have been all over his face for the entire kitchen staff to see, if any of them had happened to be looking.

'It is best to keep your mother happily occupied for as much of this weekend as possible.' He forced the words out, and forced his attention back to his dessert preparations. 'And Isabella is handling the closing at night. She can't do everything.'

Scarlett nodded. 'And you need to get on with what you're doing now. Take a break to eat, 'Renz. Promise?'

'Yes, I promise.' It would happen later, when the rush was over and before he needed to put in his final effort on his meal prep. He would take Scarlett with him and make her eat, too.

Or maybe you should focus on your work and forget all about Scarlett, who is no doubt capable of ensuring that she eats food, all by herself.

With a stifled sigh, Lorenzo got back to work.

'They're ready for you out front. Right now the cameras are on the MC while she counts this down to the entry of you, and Sorella's chef, out there.' Scarlett spoke the words in a quiet, almost awe-struck tone as she looked at the five finished desserts Lorenzo had before him. 'You've done an amazing job, Lorenzo. I don't see how those can't win tonight's part of the contest.'

Lorenzo was pleased with his efforts, too, but still cautious. 'That will depend on what the Sorella chef has prepared. I've tried for things that I'm guessing he wouldn't risk making, and yet I've stuck to traditional Italian desserts. Every dessert could be offered on our menu at any time. I think that's a good standard to stick to.'

'And a great way to get our guests trying some new dishes that we *can* add to the menu if they prove popular.' Scarlett was impressed, and didn't hesitate to show it.

The man behind the camera called for Lorenzo to get ready to take his desserts out, and counted down to the roll of the camera.

Three staff would carry the desserts. Lorenzo took up the first two, Isabella the second two, and Scarlett the final one and they all made their way through the restaurant and outside to the dais area again where the Sorella chef was also approaching.

All Lorenzo wanted, once he'd served the various desserts for the panel of judges, was to stand at Scarlett's side to wait for the results to be announced. He joined her, and Isabella excused herself to return to the kitchen.

Lorenzo let his gaze drift out over the crowded square. For a moment he thought he caught sight of a familiar figure, there at the back. His breath caught in his throat and his hand reached automatically to close around Scarlett's wrist. The protective urge that rose in him was swift and encompassing.

As he searched again, and couldn't see Marcella anywhere, he told himself it couldn't have been her. She might have interfered with his employment in the past, but she'd never visited any of the restaurants in person.

But this was Monta Correnti. She had family in this region.

You expected you might see her around the village sooner or later.

Lorenzo drew a deep breath and tried to shake the unease aside. Marcella couldn't do anything to him. He'd been as open as he could be with Luca when he had applied to work here. Luca would not sack him on Marcella's say-so, no matter what rumours she tried to set into the older man's ears.

Yes, but what if Marcella crossed paths with Scarlett? Used words to try to hurt Scarlett? Verbally bullied her or…worse? What if Marcella approached him while he was with Scarlett, and…shamed him with one of her…attacks?

But it was equally likely that Marcella was *not* in the crowd, and, if she was, how likely was it that she would make a scene here, in the midst of her family's hometown?

Lorenzo told himself it wasn't that likely, but his fingers still slid to Scarlett's hand and tightened protectively over it. She squeezed right back and he realised she probably thought he'd taken her hand due to suspense over the outcome of this round of the contest.

Within the crowd, people were oohing and aahing over the desserts as the judges tasted each one. Lorenzo released his hold on Scarlett's hand and did his bit to describe the dishes into the microphone when asked.

He tried to concentrate on the judges' comments, but all he could realise was that he was getting way too attached to having Scarlett around again. She'd stepped up to replace his missing kitchen hand, and had worked tirelessly all afternoon, stopping only once to force him to take a break and eat. Lorenzo had wanted to be successful, not only for himself and for Rosa, but also for her.

'And we're pleased to announce that the winner of tonight's round is chef Lorenzo Nesta, of Rosa restaurant.'

Scarlett made a pleased sound beside him and impulsively hugged him.

His hands automatically caught her, held her close. It took all of his focus not to dip his head and kiss her. Not because they'd won a round, though that was great and a reward for a lot of hard work, but because Scarlett was in his arms beaming from ear to ear and looking into his eyes, not only with happiness and relief, but also with affection.

'Well, done, Lorenzo.'

'You have done Rosa proud.'

The words came from Isabella and Luca. Lorenzo released Scarlett and received a kiss on each cheek from a beaming Isabella, and the same again from Luca, and then their MC was talking the crowd through what would follow for the final day's festivities.

The next half-hour passed in a blur that turned into another hour as Lorenzo returned to the kitchen with Scarlett and they both pitched in again to take care of their dinner crowd, many of whom wanted to try the winning desserts.

'It was helpful to us for the panel to make this a bulk quantity event,' Scarlett said. 'We can put the dishes on offer for all our patrons.'

That one comment of Scarlett's rang in Lorenzo's ears and then more time passed until finally the last meal was served and it was only coffees remaining, and Scarlett came to him with a bossish glint in her eyes. 'You're finishing now. There's nothing that needs doing here that we can't all manage without you.'

There were smudges beneath Scarlett's eyes. Lorenzo guessed if he looked in a mirror he'd see the same. It *had* been a big day, but for both of them, not just for him. On a night like this, he would get on his motorcycle—

'I'll go now.' He murmured it quietly. 'But you should leave too. You also need to rest.'

He didn't give Scarlett a chance to argue the point. Instead, Lorenzo turned to Isabella and caught her attention. 'Are you okay to finish up?'

'Oh, yes. You've done enough.' She gestured around her. 'We're fine here, though I'm guessing Scarlett will want a good explanation for why Rocco didn't turn up for his shift.'

'Yes, but Scarlett covered for him very well.'

And Isabella had kept Scarlett's mother occupied, and they'd now got through two events without Luca and Lisa aggravating each other.

Lorenzo led Scarlett away, not through the front, but out of the rear door. His motorcycle was beside the restaurant van.

'Are we dodging the crowds?' Scarlett tipped her face up. 'That breeze is nice. It gets a bit stuffy in the kitchen after a while.'

'I was going to offer to drop you home, but come for a ride with me. It will be a chance to blow the cobwebs away. We don't have to go far.' He drew the helmet from the handgrip and raised his brows. It was an impulsive suggestion, perhaps born out of his tiredness, and yet the idea of a late-night motorcycle ride really did appeal, and he'd like to share that with her.

Scarlett hesitated. 'You've only got one helmet.'

'There's a spare in the van.' It was Lorenzo's previous one, a little aged. He'd tossed it behind the seat there when he replaced it with this one. He quickly unlocked the van, retrieved the helmet.

'All right. I will.' The start of a smile broke over Scarlett's face as she put the helmet on. She left the visor pushed up. 'I want to feel the breeze.'

They climbed onto his motorcycle. Scarlett tucked her skirt about her legs. Her arms came around his waist and he glanced over his shoulder just as she spoke in a jesting tone. 'I hope your skills have improved since I first knew you. I'd rather you didn't tip us off into a ditch.' The skin around her eyes crinkled as she smiled. 'You were a bit clumsy, always getting scratched and bruised from taking spills on your bike. I used to worry about you really getting hurt one day but I haven't seen a mark on you since I've been back, not even that day at the pool.'

She seemed to realise that her words might sound a little too aware, a little too intimate, and fell abruptly silent.

Lorenzo fought for a calm response. Those scratches and bruises—God, he didn't want to think about it. 'I'm good on the motorcycle. Ah, now, I mean. You'll be completely safe, I promise.'

Lorenzo fired up the motorcycle and rode them away. Away from Rosa, away from crowds, away from all of it including his thoughts. He rode them out onto the hilly roads beyond the village. He rode and the cooler evening air whipped at his chef's shirt while Scarlett's warmth pressed against his back and after a while she let out a yell of pure delight, and dark memories left him and he laughed aloud.

The roads were deserted and he drove for ten minutes until Scarlett tugged on his arm and gestured for him to pull over. He came to a stop on a grassy area that led to an elevated outcrop.

Scarlett pulled her helmet off and blinked hard. 'Sorry. I think I got some dust in my eye. It's stinging. I suppose I should have put the visor down, but that breeze was worth it!'

'Let me help you.' There was a moon overhead. He drew a clean handkerchief from his trouser pocket and gently wiped her eye with it.

'I think you got it.' Scarlett blinked again.

He glanced at the white handkerchief. 'I see a black smudge.'

'Well, I'm glad we got it out. Thanks.' Scarlett turned to look out over the grassy knoll. 'It's beautiful here. You can see right out over the valley. And it's so quiet.' Her gaze rose to the sky and she drew a deep breath. 'I'm lucky. I've lived in two of the most beautiful countries of the world.'

'Australia and Italy.' He nodded. 'From when you were here…before, I think you found both countries felt like home in their ways.'

'Both did, and sometimes neither did.' Scarlett's brows drew together as she fell silent. After a moment, she went on. 'It can be hard, feeling the pull of two countries. Well of people within two countries. I'm not sure it's the land so much, as—'

'As family.' All of Lorenzo's family lived within Italy. His parents were still in the village, holding their heads up and pretending their son's marriage wasn't a farce reduced to a useless piece of paper and Marcella's long-term bitterness. Their pride and judgement hadn't helped in his situation, though he couldn't blame them too much. They only knew half the circumstances. Lorenzo could never tell them all of it.

'Yes.' Scarlett bit her lip. 'Well, I'm trying to get along with all of the family this time. Sometimes I feel like Mamma doesn't make it easy, but we've never been close. Jackie says we're too similar, but I don't want to be just like my mother. I want to be me.'

As Scarlett uttered these words to Lorenzo she acknowledged that there had been long stretches of time in her life when she would have seemed cold even to those closest to her.

Her time with Lorenzo had been different. She'd let him right into her heart, had opened parts of herself to him that she'd never trusted to anyone else.

Tonight, standing here beneath this moon with Lorenzo's gaze on her, Scarlett could almost believe—

A leaf rustled from a tree and fluttered into her face. Lorenzo reached with gentle fingers to brush it away. His hand lingered, and somehow Scarlett's cheek was pressed into the palm of his hand and, oh, she just wanted to stay like that. Her eyes drifted half closed.

'What are we doing, Lorenzo?' She whispered the words.

'I think we're doing this.' His head bent to hers until their lips met softly, so softly.

A gentle kiss in the moonlight. That was all this was. Scarlett told herself this and gave into the moment, denying everything. All her fears and worries, all of their past.

How did this happen to her? How did she yield to him in her life where she had stood firm, stood alone very often and refused, oh, so totally refused to allow anyone all the way into...her soul? Yet with this man, who had hurt her and whom she shouldn't be able to trust at all, Scarlett...let go.

And she did, and this gentle kiss became another and another until senses and yielding were all that Scarlett could feel or comprehend and somehow they were lying on the grass and

Lorenzo's breath fell on her neck before he pressed kisses there and murmured low words to her in their native language.

He murmured of his need for her and that he had missed her touch, missed her, and then he cut those words off and his mouth came to hers once again and this kiss was different. The thought crossed her mind to wonder if Jackie had felt like this when she gave herself to her young lover, and Scarlett pushed aside guilt and family too and her hands rose to clasp the sides of Lorenzo's strong neck. Her fingers splayed through the hair at his nape as he deepened their kiss and she went with him. Scarlett just…packed away everything and went with him.

The tensions of today, and yesterday, left her while she was in Lorenzo's arms. When they drew back a little and she searched his face, his eyes, there was such desire and need there and she felt it, too, deep within herself in parts of her that Scarlett had thought she had lost to love five years ago.

When her body became boneless and pliant against his, chest-to-chest, arms about each other, how could anything else happen but for them to nestle closer and kiss each other again?

Legs tangled, mouths meshed. The sky was so vast over their heads and so she blocked it out and only looked at Lorenzo's face above hers, and when even that was too much Scarlett closed her eyes and thought she should regain some control, some grip.

But then she simply felt more. Felt every sensation as their tongues brushed, as his fingers threaded into her ponytail and somehow her hair was loose about her shoulders and he'd taken her ribbon and tucked it into his shirt pocket over his chest.

Scarlett felt the warm solid press of his medallion against *her* chest, and knew there would be a faint mark there. Lorenzo held her hair in his hands and she *felt* his sensual pleasure in the touch of that silky mass through his fingers as he sighed and kissed her again.

Again and again and again.

Scarlett could have stepped over the edge into lovemaking so easily with him in those moments. She wasn't sure what stopped her, what made her thoughts come back to her, take hold of her once again so that she surfaced enough from this, from wonderful sensations and warmth and rightness to *question* that rightness.

'Lorenzo.' The word was acknowledgement, withdrawal, regret rolled into one. And self-protection. 'This can't happen.'

She eased away from his mouth, away from his arms. Oh, it was the most difficult thing Scarlett had done in a very long time.

He sat up, too, and they shared one long, silent glance before Lorenzo's expression seemed to clear and change.

Scarlett searched those changes, wanted, no, *needed* to know what they meant, what he was thinking. And she felt panicked, because why did this matter so much to her? Why did Lorenzo matter so much to her when she had fought so hard to get over him mattering, to forget him mattering? To never let him or any other man ever matter to her to that same depth again?

Scarlett didn't want that kind of hurt again. Her sister had suffered hurt. Scarlett wasn't dealing with that very well. And now she wasn't dealing with this. She felt trapped by her own tangled emotions. Trapped and yet deep inside herself she had known she needed to come back.

Not only to Italy but to Monta Correnti, to the heart of her family and to the heart of where she'd fallen for a man, and been hurt by that love, and walked away and taken herself far away and sworn not to trust again.

How did she reconcile trust with keeping herself safe? Was

that even possible? And…could she be falling back in love with him again?

You could if you wanted to. It wouldn't have to be the same now. 'You're free now.'

She didn't mean to utter the words aloud.

And she saw him stiffen. 'Scarlett—' For one moment, he looked tortured.

And Scarlett felt uncertain again for nebulous reasons, ones she couldn't pin down, and it was late and suddenly the exhaustion was all there again, only more so now because of this.

Scarlett felt scared of her own emotions. 'Please, can we go back? I'm so tired.'

Emotionally drained, physically weary. Uncertain in heart and head. For Scarlett, who needed to feel in control to feel safe, these were not good things.

No, they really were not. She got to her feet and walked on shaking legs towards Lorenzo's motorcycle.

He followed, and he opened his mouth to speak again but Scarlett just couldn't.

She shook her head and he frowned, but he got them organised and took her back into town. The square was quiet now. Scarlett refused to wonder how long they'd been gone. Lorenzo stopped his motorcycle a little away from Scarlett's lodgings and she climbed off and he put her helmet away and they walked the remainder of the way.

When they stopped outside her door she tried. Maybe it was ridiculous, almost farcical, but she had to try. 'The contest part of tomorrow shouldn't be quite as demanding for you.'

Work. The goals of Rosa. 'I appreciate how hard you've worked for Rosa, Lorenzo, and that you've been a good sport about something that started out as a small suggestion and has turned into something a lot more demanding.'

'The restaurant is fully booked again for tomorrow night.'

He seemed to want to regain that normality, too. 'It's good. What's happening for Rosa is good.'

And yet he also looked unhappy and...uneasy?

'Goodnight, Scarlett.' He stepped back from her, stepped back and turned on his heel as though he had to. 'I'll—I'll see you tomorrow at the restaurant.'

He walked away, and Scarlett went inside, and wondered if maybe she *should* have stayed at her mother's place, because at least then she might not have felt so comfortable about coming and going with Lorenzo and might have saved herself from tonight, and the questions it had raised that she had been trying very hard not to hear.

One question above all others.

She couldn't be falling for him all over again? Really falling? As in, giving-her-heart falling?

Could she?

CHAPTER NINE

'SCARLETT—' Isabella drew a breath and her hand came to rest on Scarlett's arm. 'I've been talking to Jackie and, well, I think... I think we need to talk. Will you come into Luca's office for a minute?'

It was Sunday. The restaurant was crowded with diners inside and out. Lorenzo and the Sorella chef were back at their outside cooking stations. Less than an hour from now the overall winner for the weekend would be decided, one way or another. The challenge was five authentic Italian main meals. Scarlett was convinced that Lorenzo would win this.

There hadn't been time today for even a moment alone with him, and Scarlett admitted that she had wanted, had hoped for that.

Last night...they could have ended up making love. Oh, the way she felt when she was with him! The way everything within her longed—

After five years of not seeing him, of telling herself she was over him, that the hurt he had done to her could never be forgiven and would never be forgotten. After all that, for her to still feel like herself, but also part of a bigger whole that was not just made up of her when they were together.

Surely that feeling must be rare? Surely it must mean something that was worth looking at, worth reaching for?

Scarlett had needed to look into his eyes today and see there the same expressions she had believed she saw last night on a moon-limned hilltop. Scarlett needed to feel reassured that she wasn't the only one experiencing this pull towards him. She needed to know that Lorenzo felt this, too, that he was equally involved in whatever these feelings were.

'Is it urgent, Izzie? There's a lot of patrons to look after right now and the contest is drawing to a close.' She glanced again at the packed square.

Normally Scarlett wouldn't think of anything but the work. She was a good financial manager, she knew her stuff, and she knew the importance of being aware of everything that went on in any establishment she worked in, from the ground up. Yet right now Scarlett could have turned her attention from all of it and simply spent that time looking into Lorenzo's eyes.

Well, he was busy trying to win the cook-off for Rosa. The last thing he needed was Scarlett distracting him and with that in mind she *had* stayed out of his way as much as possible so far today.

It just might have been nice to get more than one brief glance, loaded with suppressed passion and awareness though that one glance had been. Scarlett needed his touch. The feel of his arms around her, the press of his lips against hers. Words, to hear soft words spoken in her ear, pouring out his need for her as he had done last night.

You are in so deep, Scarlett. Have you thought about that?

'It's important enough.' Izzie's words were restrained. But also tense.

Scarlett searched her cousin's face and truly became aware of that tension within Izzie.

'Is this about the restaurant, Izzie? Work? The contest?' Scarlett had thought about the contest, about where it had taken Rosa and where Rosa needed to get in order to truly stay financially viable. There were possibilities nipping at the edges of her mind. She just hadn't had the time to really work them through in her thoughts.

Izzie shook her head. 'It's not really about any of those things. It's, well, it's about you. In a way. Scarlett, can we just talk? Please?'

'Yes, of course.' Scarlett's tummy did a big, uneasy flutter. 'I'm sorry, Isabella. I was distracted.' *Thinking about Lorenzo and a future I should not even be hinting at, not even in the darkest recesses of a mind that should be focused on problem solving during these working hours.* 'By, um, I was distracted by the final leg of the contest. I'll come now. Lead the way.'

It took minutes for them to make their way through the crowds. A couple of times people stopped Isabella for a short conversation. Izzie showed perfect professionalism, listening, chatting, but also winding things up quickly.

Scarlett's unease hiked with each passing moment, even as she appreciated the rapport that Isabella had with many of the diners. That rapport had to be worth something. The familiarity of a locally owned and run restaurant.

Had Luca hired Lorenzo as chef with that in mind when his previous chef moved out of the area? Knowing that people would appreciate that they were being catered for by a local man? Lorenzo had worked in other places, but he'd grown up here. His parents still lived here. Scarlett had seen them in passing though she hadn't ever met them.

Lorenzo didn't seem to speak about his family. In fact, Scarlett somehow guessed that his personal life was something that *didn't* get discussed here at Rosa.

You were his guilty secret five years ago.

That could be very different now.

Last night as she lay unable to sleep, Scarlett had finally asked herself, truly, was she falling in love with Lorenzo again? She'd tried to look at the question rationally, to examine it and assess it the way she would anything in her business world.

Instead she had simply longed for him with an ache that seemed to come right out of her soul. And when she did try to look at the whole picture, their past, the hurt, she kept coming back to... She had changed, and Lorenzo had changed. Didn't that mean that their lives were not the same now as they had been then? And if he truly made her feel this way then why should she hold back?

No, she couldn't say she was falling in love with him again. That would be a huge undertaking, would involve so much trust and she wasn't sure if she could give that trust ever again. But a part of Scarlett no longer ruled out...something?

Did she want a second affair with him now, while she was here in Italy working at Rosa? Was that the conclusion for these thoughts? These feelings? And if so, what happened after that? What happened when Rosa was back on its feet and/or Scarlett had done all that she possibly could for the restaurant and perhaps Luca said thank you, that's enough now and let her go?

Did she return to Australia and pick up the threads of her life there and forget about Lorenzo for a second time?

Like you forgot the first time?

Scarlett wasn't sure she could let herself think about the alternative, that her emotions might be on the way to getting deeply involved again. Could a woman fall in love with a man twice? And have things work out better the second time?

Well, right now she needed to deal with Isabella. Scarlett turned to face her cousin inside this small office with the door closed for their privacy. 'What is it, Izzie?'

Whatever her cousin had to say, Scarlett would rather hear it and deal with it. 'If this is about family—Jackie's photos—' Scarlett had planned to look at those, truly. At the end of tonight she would look at them. She just...

Had been avoiding doing that, and had blamed their busy work schedule for it.

Nothing was simple, was it?

'It's not about Jackie or…Kate.' Isabella's brows drew together. 'Though that's another issue that has been on my mind, Scarlett. You do need to look at Kate's photos. I think that will help you to let her be a real person to you.'

'She is real!' Scarlett bit the words off while her heart said that was the whole problem. Kate had always been a real person, first a child and now a young woman who'd had feelings and a heart and who must have spent years wondering why she'd been given up by her birth mother.

Whether she'd been happy with her adopting family or not, Kate must have experienced those thoughts, and Jackie must have longed for the daughter she lost. Scarlett's actions had forged that young woman's life path, and a lot of Jackie's, too.

'What do you need to say to me, Izzie?'

Sounds of the restaurant's busyness carried through the closed door, and the MC for the event had started the ten-minute countdown! They shouldn't stay in here for even five more minutes so whatever this was, Scarlett would rather hear it now. In an action that was perhaps reminiscent of her mother, Scarlett tightened her shoulders and stood very straight and waited to take this, whatever it was, squarely on the chin and deal with it. 'Spill, Isabella.'

'Scarlett, I saw you…looking at Lorenzo earlier.' Isabella wrung her hands once before she caught Scarlett's glance and gave a slight shake of her head. 'Looking at him as…a lover would. If I misinterpreted I hope you'll forgive me, and I know it isn't my business anyway, but it's not the first time I've intercepted something between you both and Jackie noticed it, too.'

'Well, it isn't your business, really.' The words emerged

before Scarlett had time to think about them. They emerged out of her surprise that Isabella would comment on such a thing. This was so far from what she had expected, and, really, so what?

Why would Isabella feel worried or concerned or upset about that, and enough that she would pull Scarlett out of a busy restaurant and away from the end of the contest to talk to her? 'Is this because I'm the financial manager here? You're concerned about something happening between me as I stand in that position, and another employee here?'

Fair enough if Isabella *was* concerned. Scarlett herself would have frowned on it if she'd discovered a similar situation between two staff members. And Isabella had worked with all her heart and effort for Rosa for a lot of years up to the point when Scarlett had stepped into the role of Financial Manager. But again, surely that could have waited a little?

Scarlett drew a breath and told herself to tread carefully. She and Lorenzo hadn't actually done anything that could be in any way construed as inappropriate. Well, they'd kissed beside the van, but she was confident no one had seen that. Even so, Isabella had noticed Scarlett's interest in Lorenzo and must have been truly confident in its existence to bring this up.

'It's not really about that.' Isabella shook her head. 'It's probably not the most advisable thing for two people who work together to become involved but that's life. It happens. Of course you can do whatever you want to in terms of personal relationships, Scarlett.' Isabella bit her lip. 'I'm doing a bad job of this.'

She paced away a few steps and swung around to face Scarlett again. 'It's just, I don't want you to get hurt.'

Scarlett didn't want that, either, and opened her mouth to say so, or reassure her cousin somehow, or something. 'It's kind of you to care, Izzie. I appreciate it. I truly do. But in the end, isn't it my—?'

'He's married, Scarlett.' Isabella blurted the words and fell abruptly silent. She drew a breath. 'He's married. It's just, he lives here now and his wife has a home in another, larger village and maybe they haven't actually lived together for a long time. But some couples do live apart yet are still together, if you know what I mean. Lorenzo is a great guy, but he's close-mouthed about his personal life, but I do know that much. That he is a married man.'

'Married.' The word reverberated through Scarlett's mind, echoed in her ears and…brought a tight pain to the centre of her chest. *Still married?* She struggled to comprehend.

Her gaze locked with Isabella's. She wasn't sure if she was looking for reassurance, an anchor, or some way to prove that Isabella had this all wrong.

Married.

Lorenzo Nesta was still *married.*

The fact of it started to penetrate. And a rush of memories came with her beginnings of understanding.

He'd told her five years ago that he would leave his wife. That he wanted to build a life with Scarlett. It had taken time for him to confess his marriage in the first place and by then Scarlett had been deeply in love with him. She'd made the commitment to stick with him and he had made the commitment to leave his wife and divorce her so he could…marry Scarlett.

Oh, she'd had such dreams and Lorenzo had stomped all over those dreams and now she'd come back and he'd let her care about him all over again. Let her give her kisses to him again. He'd allowed her to let him into her emotions again. Anger started somewhere deep inside Scarlett. Hurt welled, too. She tried to stopper the hurt back.

'I put it off. I didn't want to say anything—' There was

utterly no judgement in Isabella's expression or tone, just care. She wasn't accusing Scarlett of anything. She wanted to keep her cousin safe from hurt and so she'd crossed a line, risking being told it was none of her business.

Scarlett understood all of this, felt it go into her heart as an offering even as she battled to comprehend the rest and that boil of feeling continued to build.

How could Lorenzo still be married? He'd allowed her to reach out to him, to develop affection for him a second time when he'd *known* how much the last time had hurt her.

She shouldn't have let herself care. Not about him. Not… again. Had he thought she knew? But even if he did think that, she'd said out loud, 'You're free now.' He hadn't corrected her.

For a moment Scarlett felt as though she'd been thrown back through time. Except this time Scarlett hadn't fallen in love with Lorenzo. Oh, no, she had not. The anger welling up, drowning out everything else, proved that. *Anger.* Any pain was from…feeling embarrassed at being caught making a mistake like this, even if Izzie didn't know the half of it!

No. There was no love for Lorenzo. Oh, she had wondered whether she was developing *some* feelings again for him, but Scarlett was too smart to have let that happen again. And… too good at protecting herself from caring to that degree.

Stick to the point, Scarlett. 'You know this for a fact, Izzie?'

Scarlett had to make certain of that, because when she confronted Lorenzo—

'Yes, I know.' Isabella's face softened as she stepped forward and briefly touched Scarlett's arm. 'Please don't be offended that I brought this up.'

'I'm not offended, Isabella.' Scarlett could have wished that her cousin hadn't noticed her interest in Lorenzo, but she couldn't do anything about that now. All she could do was go forward and the best way to do that was to be armed with facts. 'I presume you know this from a reliable source?'

'His parents speak of the marriage as though it's only a matter of time until there'll be a full reconciliation.' Izzie gave a shrug that didn't manage to hide the careful way she examined Scarlett's face. 'I'm not at all sure that will be the case, but the fact of Lorenzo's marriage also came up one day when I was speaking to Papa. It was soon after he hired Lorenzo. He said that Lorenzo told him of the marriage himself when he applied for the job here.'

Isabella paused. 'Papa didn't say much about it, just to take Lorenzo on his own merits.' She shrugged. 'He's been a good chef, good worker, easy to get along with and fully behind the restaurant.'

And for that reason Isabella probably didn't want any waves between Scarlett and Lorenzo, either.

She wouldn't get them. Not on restaurant time, anyway. Scarlett would do her duty and be utterly professional about it, no matter if it killed her. But Lorenzo—

Yes, the issue of Lorenzo would have to be dealt with, but first there was the issue of a cousin who stood watching her and looking worried.

Scarlett took her turn to pat Isabella's arm, and gave her a smile that she hoped appeared calm. 'Thank you for telling me this and I want you to know that I'm fine. I will take care of myself. You don't need to worry about a thing, but it means a lot to me that you cared.'

And it did. 'Now, we need to get back out to the restaurant and see the rest of this evening through, and don't forget there's a celebration for the staff when we've got the dinner patrons all squared away. Everyone's worked so hard this weekend and we got a great result for Rosa. It's important to acknowledge that whether it's an overall win in the end, or not.'

Scarlett stepped ahead of Isabella out of the office. She took each step in full management mode. As she reached the dining area her gaze scanned tables, checked faces to gauge mood, contentment, looked at meals and checked the performance of staff.

This, Scarlett knew how to do, and would do with all of her might.

Never let them see your pain.

She'd heard her mother say that to a friend on the phone many years ago in a moment Scarlett had later looked back on and realised had probably shown a rare depth of honesty and introspection from Lisa.

No person was made of total stone. Not Scarlett's mum. Not Scarlett. But Scarlett could make a damned good effort at keeping her focus on her work and *acting* like stone until she got her anger under control and could face Lorenzo calmly and tell him calmly, just what she thought of him.

Yes, that was how Scarlett wanted to handle this issue. Her discussion with Lorenzo would have to wait until the end of the night. So be it. Scarlett had other things to focus on now and, anyway, it wasn't as if she was heartbroken over Lorenzo like the last time. Oh, she was not. She was so, totally not!

And if she remembered that he'd been trying to tell her something last night, and wondered if he'd intended to confess about his marriage, well, even if that was the case, it was rather late in the piece, wasn't it?

Scarlett glanced towards her cousin and opened her mouth to announce…something businesslike. Anything, really. But Isabella was staring with her eyes narrowed into the outdoor Sorella seating area. A moment later Isabella's hand closed over Scarlett's forearm.

They spoke simultaneously.

'*Rocco.*'

'It looks like he's out for a party night,' Scarlett observed quietly.

'I'll give him party-mode,' Isabella declared with a snap of her teeth. 'How dare he miss his shift and then turn up eating and drinking at Sorella the day after without a word of explanation?' She charged forward through the tables.

Scarlett, perforce, followed her cousin. She didn't even glance towards Lorenzo's workstation. And Scarlett was proud of *that*.

'You're on probation for three months.' Scarlett's words to yesterday's missing kitchen hand were calm, but firm.

She caught Lorenzo's glance on her as she uttered them. Lorenzo's expression suggested he wasn't quite sure of Scarlett's mood. He should be thankful that she could fake a level of self-possession for moments like this. She didn't exactly want to deal with Rocco right now, but, by God, she would do what she had to.

'But I told you I had a headache. A terrible headache. I still have it.'

'I don't doubt you have one *now*.' Scarlett shook her head. 'I told all the staff here when I first took over as Financial Manager that this restaurant needed to function as a team with all team members doing their utmost to support the overall effort.'

She let her gaze rake the man. 'You were needed this weekend, you made no effort to contact the restaurant to explain your absence, then we discover you in the crowd eating at Sorella, without so much as an explanation of your absence yesterday. One more misstep will result in you being fired. Are we clear?'

Scarlett stared at the man and he glared at her.

To her left, Lorenzo seemed to bristle with tension. The contest was being decided even now, but the judges had explained the final deliberations could take a while and Lorenzo had obviously spotted the situation with Rocco and come to offer his presence in the way of some reinforcement.

Not that Scarlett and Isabella couldn't have got Rocco into Rosa by themselves, Scarlett told herself, and utterly disregarded the fact that Rocco had been recalcitrant until Lorenzo had walked over to join them and backed Scarlett's request for a few words with the man.

As it was, Rocco had barged into the kitchen rather than going to the office.

'Whatever you say.' The hand spoke the words sarcastically and turned away.

Unfortunately as he walked towards the doors of the kitchen Scarlett heard the rather pointed curses he uttered. They were about her, and vile enough to drain the blood from her face for a moment before she pulled herself together.

Lorenzo also heard, and he came forward before Scarlett could move.

'You just stepped over the line.' He addressed the man and gestured to the doors. 'I've warned you about skipping shifts twice before, but this…is beyond tolerable. Scarlett has been too generous to you and I don't mind stepping in to say this, to save her from wasting her breath on you. You're fired. Leave, and do it through the rear doors away from the patrons. If there's pay owing to you, it'll be mailed.'

The man looked disbelieving for a moment. He swayed on his feet. He was more inebriated than he'd looked.

Well, if Lorenzo hadn't uttered those words, Scarlett would have. Yet she didn't want to see Lorenzo's strength right now. Scarlett didn't want to be conscious of him at all in any way, but…at least Rocco was being dealt with. Scarlett stifled a sigh.

'Fine, I'm going.' The guy shoved the doors open and stumbled out. 'I didn't like working here anyway. I'd rather be in one of the big cities where there's actually some life!'

As he left, Lorenzo glanced at two of the other hands. 'Make sure he leaves, please.'

The two hands walked out behind Rocco.

Scarlett drew a deep breath. 'Well, that's done.' She glanced at Lorenzo but didn't let herself meet his gaze. 'You need to get back to your station. The results could come in at any moment.'

Lorenzo hesitated before he said, 'After the contest I think we need—'

'To speak. Yes. After the contest, when this night is over.' There would be a reckoning. Perhaps Lorenzo understood that. Scarlett hoped she could pull herself together a little between now and then.

And Scarlett tried.

And to a degree, she succeeded.

Enough that she felt genuine excitement and happiness when the announcement came that the contest was over, and Rosa had won!

The staff finished serving everyone, and cleared the restaurant out. Scarlett was thrilled for the restaurant, grateful to Lorenzo for his work, and still furious at him and hurt, so hurt, all rolled into one.

But she had a job to do, and she pitched in to help with the final clean-up, and once it was done she gathered the staff together in the kitchen and gave her congratulatory speech to everyone. She could do this. She would do this. She wasn't Lisa Firenzi's daughter for nothing, and right now Scarlett was claiming every bit of her mother's strength and using it to keep herself afloat. 'Thank you all. You've made a wonderful effort, I'm so proud.'

She hesitated and then forged on. 'We've had our moments this weekend and I know some of that has probably been a bit off-putting for you all, too. I appreciate your professionalism and that you all just got on with your work.'

Lorenzo listened to Scarlett's words and felt such a mix of emotions. He pushed back the healthy weariness of several very busy days, and focused his attention on Scarlett. He couldn't pin down all of what was bothering her, but he knew her and his need to be private with her and, he wasn't sure, *find out what was amiss,* was roaring at him. It was more than Rocco missing a shift and being rude.

Taking that situation into account and whatever else was upsetting Scarlett, she had gone on to work professionally. Her ability to handle herself so well in such management issues showed her strength, and yet hers was a very different kind of strength from…Marcella's.

He pushed the thought aside, but unease remained. Scarlett *was* too calm. As though beneath the surface something bubbled and all her attention was focused on controlling it, not letting others see it.

'So a heartfelt three cheers for a magnificent effort this weekend to our fabulous head chef, and to all of you who worked so hard to help him achieve this win!'

Scarlett applauded. The other staff members applauded and cheered and beamed. Luca was here, too, though he'd missed the drama earlier and perhaps that was for the best. He also applauded and cheered and beamed.

'Speech, Lorenzo.'

'Yes, speech, speech!'

'Thank you.' Lorenzo let his gaze drift over the group. There was only one gaze he wanted to meet but she didn't want to allow it right now and in truth now wasn't the time. He went on. 'This was a team effort and whether we ended up winning or not it still would have been a highly successful weekend. It was great to see the square packed and our tables packed.'

'Yes, and let's keep up the good work.' Scarlett added these final words before she said, 'First thing tomorrow. For now, we deserve a glass of wine before we all go home to rest!'

There was cake, too, baked by Isabella and brought in especially. While Isabella handed pieces of that around, Scarlett poured wine with a rock-steady hand.

Even now her face was pleased, encouraging, appropriately proud of the staff and their work—including Lorenzo's. On the surface, nothing looked amiss. So why did Lorenzo feel so concerned?

But he was. Last night, he and Scarlett had almost made love. He had needed her with such depth within himself and yet his life was not the uncomplicated thing that he wished it could be.

Luca knew about Marcella. Oh, not all of it. Lorenzo would never, ever tell the truth of that, not to a soul. How could he when his shame burned so deep even now? But he had explained about past job problems from his wife, that they lived separately, the bare minimum for a man who had wanted to know how Lorenzo would fit back into the Monta Correnti community.

Mostly Lorenzo had tried to do so quietly. He'd rented a small home and got on with it.

Lorenzo remembered last night. Holding Scarlett in his arms. Had it been their surroundings that had affected him that way? The darkness, the time of night, the moon shining over them or the quietness and rest of that moment that had made him long so much to make her his once again?

Or perhaps it had simply been Scarlett, and him, for hadn't the two of them always been like that? Hadn't he needed her with a need that had surpassed everything? Wasn't that why things had ended up as they did? Because he had wanted her, needed her, despite every complication? He'd made promises and not kept them and Scarlett had gone back to Australia hurting. If Marcella again discovered he was seeing Scarlett, Lorenzo didn't know what harm she might try to do.

He *had* to tell Scarlett. About Marcella. How things were for him now. The thought made him sick. To admit to Scarlett that Marcella had used her vicious tongue against him to the point that he had been let go from other restaurants would be bad enough. What kind of man let that happen to him? And that was the least of it.

The pride of generations warred inside Lorenzo with the need to be fair to Scarlett, to try to find some way with her, and yet he hadn't found a way the last time and in the end what had changed? Nothing, but if he told Scarlett, then at least she would know and maybe not feel hurt—

And there he went, imagining that Scarlett would willingly *want* a second chance with him. She might have been experiencing a resurgence of an old attraction, and maybe last night had made her realise that wasn't what she wanted at all.

'Goodbye. Thanks again. See you tomorrow.' Scarlett waved the last person out of the restaurant. They'd cleaned up after their little celebration and now it was just her and Lorenzo.

'You haven't seemed yourself tonight.' His words were quiet.

She would have even said gentle.

But also uneasy somehow. Had he guessed what she had found out?

The question was enough to bring back a surge of emotion that twisted into a thick knot in her chest. A knot of anger, Scarlett assured herself, and, for the first time since Isabella had taken her into Luca's office, she let her face reveal that emotion. Well, it *was* anger and he'd earned it. She squashed any knowledge of other feelings.

He drew a breath. 'Scarlett, there's something I need to tell you. I started to last night, but—'

'Isabella told me—' She snapped her teeth together and narrowed her eyes.

Lorenzo stopped speaking, too.

And Scarlett finished it. 'You're still married. You *never* left her. Not only when you said you would back then and didn't and broke my heart, but not any time since. I had a right to know that, Lorenzo. You kissed me. We almost made love!'

'I did leave her.' He cast a tortured look her way. 'I left... as soon as you were safely back in Australia.'

Safely! She drew a sharp breath and her voice rose. 'As though you couldn't get rid of me fast enough!' Scarlett was losing her self-control and couldn't seem to do a thing about it.

'No. No!' He raised his hands, palms up. 'Please, Scarlett, if you'll let me try to explain.'

'How can you possibly explain?' Scarlett shook her head. She'd thought she needed this, to have her say, to tell him she was onto his duplicity, his deceitfulness, that she wasn't going to let him get away with hurting her all over again, but...

Scarlett was tired and her emotions were tired and she was confused and she wasn't sure she had quite the level of strength that she needed to manage this. 'There's no need to explain because the truth is out now and that's all that matters. Just stay out of my way until I'm finished here and can go back to Australia, that's all!'

She would focus on achieving the two goals that had brought her back to Italy. On making Rosa viable and successful, and on connecting with her family. Why, only this morning Izzie had said that Luca's second American son, Angelo, had been talking to his twin, Alex, and was considering a visit to Monta Correnti to meet the family. These were the things Scarlett needed to care about!

She turned to make her way to the front of the restaurant.

Let Lorenzo close up. He had to go out the back way anyway, she remembered, because one of the hands had collected him in the van today. They'd wanted some last-minute ingredient and that had made more sense, so Lorenzo was to drive the van home tonight.

None of which mattered a marinated olive to Scarlett!

'All right, then let me at least see you safely home.' Lorenzo took a step towards her.

'No, thank you!' She opened her mouth to tell him all the reasons she did not want his company.

Just as a shattering crash sounded at the front of the restaurant.

CHAPTER TEN

'WHAT was that?' As the sound of splintering glass echoed through the front part of the restaurant Scarlett caught her breath and started forward.

Lorenzo touched her arm and swore. 'That sounded like a brick or something coming through one of the windows. Wait here while I go look.'

He flung the kitchen door open and started to stride forward without waiting for a reply.

Scarlett didn't give him one. She simply started forward at his side. Upset or not, she wasn't about to let him go out there on his own.

They were both just outside the kitchen swing doors. There was a shout outside. A second missile flew through the broken window.

A bottle, a burning wick. The smell of petrol. The sound of footsteps running away.

'Oh, my God!'

'Get back, Scarlett!' As Lorenzo spoke he grasped her arms and shoved them both through the kitchen doors. The bottle exploded and there was a whooshing sound. Shards of glass hit against the doors behind them.

Lorenzo's arms were hard about her, his back to the doors.

He'd placed himself directly between Scarlett and the danger, and she didn't know—

'Are you hurt?' She pulled at his arms to try to get him to turn so she could check his back. 'Did any of it get you?'

'No, I'm not hurt.' He drew a breath. 'You're all right?'

'Yes.' And she was, and later she would have time to think about how safe he had made her feel, how utterly protected even as she had feared for *his* safety. But now—

'Stay here.' Lorenzo pushed the door enough to see flames licking all over the room. He grabbed the fire extinguisher off the wall and rushed out of the door and into the restaurant area, spraying with determined, focused control.

Scarlett grabbed the other extinguisher and followed. The fire spread so fast, balls of it everywhere where the bottle had shattered and its contents had poured out and caught fire from the burning wick.

'Be careful. Leave me to do this!' Lorenzo shouted the words at her.

'I'm not leaving you,' she shouted back.

Lorenzo cast one lightning-fast, worry-filled glance at her before he redoubled his efforts and so did she and minutes later there was foam everywhere and spattered on their hands and arms and clothes, but the fire was out.

'*Polizia* and the fire brigade! I want both.' Lorenzo barked it as he stormed into the kitchen and snatched the phone off the wall. A moment later he had someone on the line. He explained, firing off the words in rapid Italian before he slammed the phone back into its cradle.

'I have to check outside, Scarlett.' He drew a sharp breath and the look on his face…

Scarlett wanted to hold him, but instead *she* drew a breath. 'I'll come with you.'

'No, please. Not until I make sure we're safe here. Truly, Scarlett. Stay here where I don't have to worry about you.' He walked briskly away from her.

And because of the tone of his voice, the protectiveness in

it and…so much more that Scarlett couldn't find the thoughts to describe, she nodded her head. 'I have the phone. If you're not back very fast—'

But he checked, and there was certainly not anybody hanging about. They'd run, just as he and Scarlett had heard.

Even so, when he stepped back inside she started to shake and her hands reached for him. 'Wait for the police, now, and the fire brigade. They can do the rest. Don't—don't leave—'

Me. The safety of here.

'Scarlett.' He looked into her eyes for one short moment before he made a deep sound in the back of his throat and crushed her into his arms.

Where was her anger now? All Scarlett could do was hold on, hold on so tight.

Outside a siren sounded, and they broke apart to go out and meet the authorities.

The next minutes passed in a blur. Family arrived and rapidly amassed until Scarlett felt certain they must all be there. Lorenzo had called Luca. Others had come. Izzie, Jackie, Max and Romano, and some of the restaurant staff, too. Lisa was also there, a sombre, concerned Lisa who hugged her daughter and went to stand beside Luca as he frowned over the messy restaurant dining room.

Scarlett heard them speaking quietly, saw Mamma lay her hand on Luca's arm. She knew she should wade in, start planning for tomorrow, do something, but she couldn't seem to get her feet to move her away from Lorenzo's side.

'This makes me think of Cristiano.' Isabella uttered the words as she paused beside Scarlett and Lorenzo for a moment. 'The thought of my brother fighting huge blazes for a living—'

'Yes, it would be brave work.' Scarlett's glance moved to

Lorenzo. *He* had been brave, throwing himself into saving the restaurant and trying to protect her at the same time.

'Isabella?' Luca called to his daughter.

'Excuse me, Scarlett.' Isabella hurried away.

'We have to give the police formal statements, Scarlett.' Lorenzo turned from where he'd been speaking quietly with one of the officers. 'But he says tomorrow will do for that. We've given them as much information as we know for now.'

'Good. That's good.' She drew a breath. 'I should speak with Luca.'

But her uncle was already on his way to them. He wrapped Scarlett in a bear hug before he drew back. 'The floor is damaged and some of the tables are badly singed, but it could have been so much worse. Thank you both for your swift actions and I want you to go now. We can't clean up until the police have finished examining it, and they've heard your thoughts including the sacking of the kitchen hand and his anger as he left. Go and rest. Scarlett, your mamma thought you might go to her villa—'

As Luca uttered the words Lisa joined them. 'Yes, Scarlett. I was out…visiting when I got the call regarding this, but that can…wait. You're more than welcome to come. Please.'

'I appreciate it, Mamma.' Scarlett shook her head, and softened her words. 'But I'd rather go back to my bedsit. It's been…an exhausting day one way and another.'

'And my independent niece needs to handle that her own way?' Her uncle seemed to understand.

Lisa's mouth tightened and her gaze searched Scarlett's face before she seemed to relax. 'You are too like me sometimes, my girl, but if that's what you need, I understand.'

'Thanks, Mamma.' Scarlett took the brief hug her mother gave her, and squeezed back, and a moment later Lisa excused herself, got on her cell phone, and began to speak softly to someone, explaining that she would be 'back there soon'.

'That tone… Mamma must be dating someone. I wonder if he's local.' Scarlett uttered the thoughts out loud before she clamped her mouth closed.

Luca looked intrigued before he cleared his throat. 'Well, it's late. We can't do any more. My sister…' His face softened. 'Lisa has offered us as many of Sorella's outdoor dining settings as we need until this can be fixed. It's generous and so we will be fine to open tomorrow, just working around the mess until we can get that sorted.'

'I was going to speak with you about how best to manage that.' Scarlett was relieved for Rosa. And pleased to hear of this olive branch between brother and sister, too. No pun intended, she thought with an edge of slightly uncontrolled humour. Scarlett frowned. She had better not start getting hysterical! 'Is there truly nothing I can do now?'

'Nothing.' Luca shook his head. 'And I want to shoo everyone else, too. Why don't you and Lorenzo go now? Maybe that will make it easier to get others moving as well.'

Scarlett gave in and nodded.

When Lorenzo led her around to the rear of the restaurant she went without question.

He helped her into the passenger seat of the van as though she were very fragile, climbed behind the wheel and drove the short distance to stop outside her bedsit.

Her landlady was away visiting her daughter again, so the place was in darkness. Scarlett turned. She knew she had to let him go and yet she was loath—

'I know you refused your mother's offer to stay with her, but I can't let you stay here tonight, Scarlett.' His words emerged on a low tone. An unhappy tone, and one that he followed with more words as she hesitated with her hand on the door of the van ready to open it. 'We speculated with the police that it was possible this crime may have happened as a result of sacking that kitchen hand.'

He drew a breath. 'That's a guess, but whether it might be true or not, I don't want you to stay here by yourself until this is resolved. There are people who know you live here alone. I can't bear the thought of any harm coming to you.'

Scarlett drew a breath. Not because she felt frightened, but because of his care. She felt overwhelmed. She didn't know what to think any more. Right now Scarlett wasn't sure if she *could* think.

'Scarlett, please.' He drew a breath. 'I want…I need…'

Scarlett waited and for some reason her heart was in her throat. 'You…?'

He blew out a breath. 'Will you please pack a bag? I could drive you to your mother's. *I will drive you wherever you choose to go.* But…I'd like you to come to my home first. I'd like to…go over all the possibilities of who might have been behind tonight's attack on the restaurant. There are some other…options that…should be discussed, I think. I didn't know whether I should bring them up to the police, or not.'

Scarlett hadn't thought about being unsafe in her home. She wanted to say she would be just fine and yet she still felt shaken. Most of all, she didn't feel ready to let Lorenzo out of her sight yet. Scarlett had feared for his safety, too. 'I'll pack a bag. It will only take a few minutes.'

She slipped out of the van and into her bedsit without waiting for him to answer. Gathering things took even less time than that. Scarlett simply stuffed what she might need into the carry-on travel bag she'd brought on the plane with her when she first arrived from Australia, securely locked her door and rejoined Lorenzo in the van.

Why did she have this compulsive need to reach across the van's interior and clasp his hand with hers? The hug they had shared earlier had been filled with relief and yet Scarlett did not feel relieved enough. Her reactions to those events were only beginning to register and as they did so they built up inside her. She tried to push them down, to keep them all nicely and neatly tidied and under control.

She'd been so angry with him, and hurt. Fearing for his safety had stripped all that away and left only…

'I rent a place here.' As Lorenzo spoke he slowed the van and turned it into the driveway of a modest home. It was a small neat place painted white and with a garden all around. A mellow light shone on the small front porch. He glanced at her as he turned off the van. 'Ready?'

'Yes.' She clasped her travel bag and climbed out of the van. He came to join her, closed and locked the doors, clasped her hand and led the way to the door of his house.

Scarlett didn't know Lorenzo's thoughts in that moment. He might have taken her hand simply to guide her through the dim area to the door. She only knew her reactions. She felt thrown straight back through time to other occasions when he had clasped her hand in his, had held her even just in that way as though she was…his world and he never wanted to let go.

Emotion rose to clog her throat. God, it had been a bottle bomb, not really all that dangerous.

Oh, yes? If you hadn't still been there, the restaurant would have burned to the ground.

But they *had* been there and so there was the possibility that someone had hoped to burn the place down with them inside it?

'It's all right, Scarlett.' Lorenzo let them inside his home. They stepped into a small foyer and he led her straight from there to a cosy living room, flicking the light switch on as they stepped into the room.

A moment later, he'd turned, taken the bag from her hands and tossed it onto the nearest leather lounge chair, and his fingers were gently tipping up her chin. 'It's all right. You're safe.'

'I didn't need to bring my bag in.' She uttered the inanity, and then responded to his statement. 'Yes, we're safe now, and what if *you* hadn't been?' The words burst out of her and… that was the end of it.

Scarlett didn't know who reached. He did, or she did. What difference did it make? All she knew was she had her arms tight around his middle. He tucked her in against his chest, his chin resting over the top of her head as he rubbed flat, open-palmed hands over her shoulders and upper back. She felt the imprint of his medallion against her, its comforting press.

'I was the one who got that kitchen hand angry. Maybe I could have handled the conversation better.' Scarlett released her hold on Lorenzo enough to look up into his eyes as she faced her concerns, as she finally allowed all of what had happened to rise inside her. 'If I'd handled him better maybe this wouldn't have happened. What if I'd gone and you'd still been there and maybe you hadn't noticed what was happening or the fire spread differently and you couldn't get out to safety? I not only let something bad happen to Luca's restaurant while under my management, but I put you in danger.'

'No, Scarlett. No.' His fingers wrapped around hers and squeezed and he…looked tortured. 'You handled that situation exactly as it needed to be handled, and I was the one to sack him. When he spoke to you that way—'

'And now we don't know if he decided to give the restaurant what he thought *it* deserved.' Scarlett shook her head.

'It is possible.' Lorenzo drew a breath and let her hands go. He gestured behind them and they took seats beside each other on the sofa.

Scarlett was surprisingly glad to get off her feet. Her legs felt shaky! 'You say that as though you have your doubts.' It took effort to draw her thoughts together to focus on this, but it was very necessary. 'We do need to really discuss this, dig around in any possibilities. The police need whatever leads we might be able to give them.'

'I don't know what to think.' Lorenzo rubbed his hand through his hair and his mouth tightened into a flat line. 'The timing is right for this to have been done by him, but in truth it could have been any person for any reason.'

'But more than one person.' They'd heard two sets of steps running away, and something about those steps... 'One of them sounded like a woman in heels. I didn't think about that until just now!'

'But you're right.' He drew a breath.

'What is it?' Scarlett searched Lorenzo's face. There was torture there, guilt, so much guilt, just as there had been five years ago when he told her he couldn't leave his wife.

Is it guilt, Scarlett? Are you sure that's exactly what you're seeing?

Even now, she wanted to hold him even more than she wanted and needed to be held by him. Something deep inside Scarlett responded to whatever hid in the backs of Lorenzo's eyes. She needed to...comfort him. Was she being silly? Had the night's events got to her and made her over-dramatise this? Was she seeing things where there was nothing to be seen?

Lorenzo swallowed and leaned forward. 'I'm concerned that my...wife may have been behind that attack. That's part of the reason why I don't want you to go back to your bedsit tonight. If it was Marcella, she would have to be in a deep state of rage, and I can't stand the thought that she might—'

He was concerned for Scarlett's safety. That was the first thing to register. Scarlett's emotions unfurled within her, letting him back in where she had tried to lock him out when she discovered he was still married. She just couldn't seem to help that. 'Why would…Marcella do such a thing? Are you saying she might do something like that to get at you?'

'I've…lost several chef's positions thanks to Marcella's poisonous tongue. Each time I found employment, sooner or later she found out where I was working and started her campaign to undermine my employer's confidence in me.' He admitted this in a low tone. 'I don't know whether she would go this far, and I don't know whether I should tell the police of such suspicions!'

Scarlett drew a sharp breath. 'Employers shouldn't have judged you on her say-so.'

'No, but sometimes all it takes is a few hints…' He swallowed before he went on. 'I did go to her, Scarlett, five years ago. I told her about you and asked her to set me free. We still lived in the same house but our relationship was already over, had been over for some time. She knew it. She knew that, for me, there was never going to be any chance for the two of us.'

'You didn't tell me that.'

'No. You were so hurt, and I…could barely think straight at that time, either.' He went on. 'Marcella refused to release me from the marriage. She threatened recompense to me but also to you if I didn't remain with her and play the good husband to the outside world, even as we were living separate lives behind closed doors.'

A picture was forming in Scarlett's mind. A picture that didn't entirely make sense but that explained some things. He'd said he did that *soon after Scarlett went back to Australia.* 'You waited for me to be safely out of the picture and then you left her, but you haven't divorced her. That doesn't make a lot of sense.'

He got up from the sofa and took three jerky paces away from her before he swung about. 'Yes, I did walk out on her after I lost you. Her response to that was to get me fired from my job.' He'd worked in a nearby village at that time. 'For months I was scrambling to get another position and hold onto it. I was worried about money, Marcella's family *and mine* were putting the screws on me on the one hand to let her have our house, and on the other to go back to her, to make it all look right.

'I had my father and mother telling me it was all my fault because we hadn't been able to have a baby as well.' He sucked up a breath. 'All I wanted to do was—'

He stopped abruptly. 'Well, that doesn't matter now. By the time the dust settled you were gone. But Marcella has gone on with those tricks. When Luca interviewed me for this position I told him about Marcella. It was the first time I'd... admitted that to anyone and I didn't want to tell him, but I couldn't afford to keep losing jobs. I asked him to judge me on my merits, to let me prove myself at Rosa no matter what he might hear about me.'

'And then I came along and you didn't know if I would fire you out of anger over our...past.' Scarlett felt shamed now to know that the thought had gone through her mind, and that she had let Lorenzo know that she had the power to make that happen.

He'd said he and Marcella had tried to have a baby and hadn't been able to. For such a proud man, that must have been a difficult matter to face, too. 'Not everyone can have children but there are other options.'

'Maybe one day Marcella will accept that. At the time it was just one more thing she wanted to blame me for, get... angry at me about.' As he searched her face perhaps he saw something in her expression that exposed her thoughts because he said quietly, 'As far as I'm aware I'll be able to father children. It was...Marcella who had the difficulties, and even with the help of a fertility clinic she wasn't able to conceive.'

'All that must have happened—'

'Before you came into my life.' His gaze softened as he looked into her eyes. 'Marcella and I...married young. It pleased our families and I didn't see her in her true colours at first.'

What he had endured at Marcella's hands reminded Scarlett of the hurt that *she* had endured at *Lorenzo's* hands. Yet she could see now that many of his decisions back then hadn't been as simple as she had imagined them to be.

Even now, Scarlett didn't understand all of his motivations, what had driven him. Just what he'd had to deal with when it came to Marcella. 'Life is complicated, isn't it? I had no idea about any of this.'

'I don't think you would have sacked me from Rosa, Scarlett. Not on the strength of our past. I admit I was concerned about it at first, but if it had come down to it I don't think you would have been prepared to do that without a fair cause.' He stopped and his hands dropped to his sides as his gaze roved over her. 'The woman who stood at my side tonight fighting a fire to save Rosa and getting herself messed up in the process isn't someone who would be vindictive, or unfair.'

His faith humbled her. Their conversation, though it had been uncomfortable perhaps for both of them and had covered ground that *still* made Scarlett uncomfortable and clearly made him uncomfortable, too, had changed her view of past events.

Scarlett had thought mostly of herself when that all went wrong. She'd been hurting and she hadn't stopped to think of what Lorenzo might have been facing.

Life *was* complicated. People did behave in certain ways for certain reasons. Lorenzo's pride had been pricked as he spoke with her about these topics that were, to him, very personal indeed.

They had *both* suffered, and maybe she hadn't really considered that until now.

Her emotions felt shaken in that moment for altogether other reasons than the threat of a fire to Luca's beloved Rosa.

And because she did feel shaken and didn't quite know how to deal with that feeling and was only now beginning to really notice the fact that the two of them were alone in his cosy house in the middle of the night, Scarlett glanced down at her clothes and forced a grimace that she hoped would hide her deeper feelings. 'At least we got the muck off our hands.'

'Yes.' He drew a breath and his gaze caught on hers and everything she had thought and all her defences and ideas were nothing anyway.

Totally nothing.

Scarlett's breath stilled in her throat and her entire being seemed to still, to be waiting for something. Waiting...for Lorenzo? 'I think you should wait before you voice any suspicions to the police about Marcella.'

His mouth tightened. 'I *thought* I caught a glimpse of her in the crowd this weekend—not tonight—but in the end I wasn't even sure it was her.'

'Leave that until tomorrow. See what the police say, first.' Scarlett felt this was the right decision. Why expose his history to all if that turned out to be quite unnecessary?

'All right. It can wait for now.' He took a small step forward. A small step closer to her. 'We both smell of fire.'

Scarlett nodded. 'It's been a huge day.'

They were words. But with the words came a change in expression, a change in the atmosphere.

In that moment they somehow moved from trying to find answers to the crux of *all* their unanswered questions. To something that felt deeper than questions, even more necessary in this moment than answers to questions.

Finally, as though Scarlett had waited for it since he had

hugged her after they put the fire out—or perhaps she had been waiting for ever—Lorenzo's hands rose to her shoulders and gently shaped them.

Blame it on tiredness or the fears of that fire or emotional exhaustion, Scarlett didn't know. But she melted into the caress of his fingers. Her thoughts and worries and concerns all melted right along with her.

She didn't *want* to stress about any of this any more, not tonight, and something inside her just…gave way. She swallowed and her gaze fell on his mouth, and then his lips were on hers and her hands rose to his chest and she closed her eyes and took this kiss that was what she needed whether it was the worst thing she could have done, or not. Scarlett didn't know the answer to that question, either.

He kissed her gently, his lips brushing over hers again and again until Scarlett melted against him, soft feminine curves to strong, muscled male. As she melted their kisses deepened.

Scarlett surrendered and her eyelids drifted closed. 'I've needed this. I've needed it, 'Renz.'

'To hold and be held.' It was a statement, not a question. 'With *you,* Scarlett. I've needed it with you. I don't know what I'd have done if you'd been hurt tonight.' His words whispered against the side of her neck, and he sounded so torn, so worried for her, and his voice was deep and the warmth of his lips even now filled her thoughts.

Her head tilted, exposing the soft skin of her nape, silently inviting… 'We're both here. We're here, Lorenzo.'

And they were, and kisses turned to touches and caresses as they stood in the centre of that room and, one after another, softly discarded all the things that had held them apart. Their history, the hurts, all of it drifted to the floor as they removed each other's clothes. It had been so long and yet it felt like yesterday. Every touch was new, and yet familiar, awaited and already known.

When the last piece of clothing fell away he took her hand and he led her to the bathroom and that felt exactly right, as though in this moment they could also wash away the past along with the scent of the fire. Wash it aside and take this, take this moment now.

The shower ran warm and they stepped beneath the spray and Scarlett looked into his eyes until it was just them and wet hair streaming down her back and Lorenzo drying her with a fluffy towel. Finally they lay in each other's arms on soft sheets that he had slept in, that held his scent.

'Are you sure, *tesoro mia*?' At the last moment, he hesitated, seemed uncertain of his ground and of this. 'I *am* still married to her.'

'I'm sure. Tonight there's nothing, only this.' There was something else. There was the question: *Why is he still married to her?* Pride? To keep their families off his back? Because she had threatened more trouble if he divorced her? Because he'd already left her, and how much worse could a divorce be?

Scarlett did want to know, but for now he'd called her his treasure while soft brown eyes looked into hers and Scarlett had a feeling that her gaze would be equally unguarded because she was sure about this moment.

And then she just didn't care about any of that at all because all Scarlett could do was feel as he loved her with his body and the touch of his hands and a soft, giving gaze that didn't leave her, didn't waver.

He loved her and Scarlett loved him, with a unity that was as remarkable now as it had been five years ago.

No. That wasn't right. This was even more, deeper, stronger than even that had been. Scarlett, *this Scarlett,* gave all of herself to this moment with a man who was like no other in her life. He had always been...Lorenzo.

As their passion built Scarlett's heart reached for him and

her senses embraced him and all that she was needed him
so, so much.It wasn't a calm and rational choice, or even a
decision. This just *was*.

Scarlett was so beautiful, so completely giving of herself.
Lorenzo looked into her eyes and everything inside him that
had been locked away, set aside, stifled and muffled and not
allowed to live since the day she left…broke free and made
its way to her in each touch. In each moment of possession
and of giving of himself to her.

Only with Scarlett could he give and trust, give of his heart
and his body equally. This was a gift that he could give to
Scarlett, could trust to her. Was he still in love with her? He
didn't know, but he knew the need to love her and so that was
what he did until he brought them both to the edge of completion and Scarlett shattered in his arms and he shattered with
her, and words of praise and affection poured out of him and
his arms wrapped deep around her.

His hands pressed against her shoulder blades so he could
hold them heart to heart while their breathing first rushed,
and then eased, and Scarlett slumped in his arms.

He'd waited for that without realising, for that one final
moment of surrender that she had always given to him.
Lorenzo rolled gently onto his back then, his arms still around
her.

Her head rested against his chest. Her body was soft and
warm against him. He had missed her so much and not even
realised.

'I'm sleepy, 'Renz.' She murmured it against his chest. 'So
sleepy.'

He stroked his hand over her hair, brushed it away from her
neck so he could kiss her there, kiss the warm saltiness of her
skin and keep the taste on his lips as he whispered, 'I know.
Sleep. No one's expecting you tonight. We have time.'

To take this.

To let themselves have this.

Scarlett drifted into sleep and Lorenzo held her and if this had been another time he would have slept, too, but not this time. He wanted to treasure every moment of this, not lose any of it.

He needed to hold Scarlett while he thought about…the future.

Lorenzo pressed a butterfly kiss to the top of her head and faced one of his answers. He hadn't fallen back in love with her.

He'd never stopped loving her. To the depths of his being.

Where did he go with that? How could he give Scarlett all the love in his heart when his past was what it was? When his past still trapped him, even now? He hadn't told her all of it. Shame burned deep inside him, burned until Scarlett sighed in her sleep and burrowed her face into his neck and, in her sleep, murmured his name.

Lorenzo closed his eyes and the big weekend and tonight's problems and the time they had spent together here, *and* his shame, all caught up with him.

Tomorrow he would have to face all of this, figure out what to do and say and how to go forward, if going forward was even possible.

He drew a breath and he, too, slept.

CHAPTER ELEVEN

'SCARLETT, I'm sorry to wake you. It's still before dawn but I thought we'd better talk.' Lorenzo's soft words woke Scarlett. 'I brought coffee for you.'

The bed dipped as he sat on its edge.

She opened her eyes to the sight of him, fully dressed in a fine white linen shirt and black trousers. His hair was still damp. He must have taken a shower while she slept.

Scarlett remembered their shared shower last night and all that it had led to. He turned his head and their gazes met and, through eyes still blurred with sleep, she looked into familiar features.

Though she knew that she was vulnerable and her instincts were starting to warn her that she needed to do something about that, that she had *made* herself vulnerable last night, and where had that got her because he was *still*, when it came down to it, a married man? Despite these thoughts, her heart swelled.

While Scarlett lay in Lorenzo's bed and he looked down at her with gentle eyes that only as he had loved her last night had come anywhere near close to losing all their shadows, love coursed through her until it filled every part of her.

Love for Lorenzo, this man who had broken her heart and loved her so gently. Scarlett didn't want him to break her heart again and yet...

Scarlett Gibson was still in love with Lorenzo Nesta. She still wanted and needed him. Her emotions were still entangled in him. She hadn't got over him as she had thought she'd done. Rather, she was more in love with him now than she could ever remember being.

How could Scarlett feel this way when she *knew* he was still married, even if he hadn't lived as husband and wife with Marcella for over five years?

Uncertainty started to come to Scarlett then. Uncertainty that the events of last night had stifled and overruled. What did she know of Lorenzo now that made any difference to the way things had been last time? He *was* still married, and if things had been so bad with his wife why hadn't he divorced her as he had told Scarlett he would before he went back on his word?

Why leave but not get a divorce? What more could he possibly have to lose?

Maybe he hasn't felt the need. Maybe if he did, he would take care of that straight away now.

But Lorenzo had lost employment because of his wife's campaign to blacken his name each time he got a new position. What more could she do to him if he asked for that divorce?

'Drink your coffee, Scarlett.' He drew a breath and handed her a T-shirt that he held in the fist of his hand. 'You can put this on if you'd like and while we have that coffee, maybe we should…talk. I can see that, like me, you're starting to think about what happened last night. Both between us, and at Rosa.'

Did he plan to blame the one for the other? Say that the stress of fighting that fire had driven them into each other's arms?

Well, hadn't it?

In some ways, Scarlett supposed, it had. Her need to connect with Lorenzo after that fright had been strong.

But now...they had to sort themselves out. They had to deal with 'What happens next?'. Scarlett didn't have a clue what the answer was to that question.

Scarlett looked again at Lorenzo. 'We need to discuss strategy for a few things. Where the restaurant can go from here is one. And we need to contact the police and find out if they have any news to tell us.'

Yes, these things were important. And yes, Scarlett had somewhat used them as a way of avoiding other matters. Scarlett shrugged the shirt over her head beneath the sheets, and sat up. All she really wanted to do was reach for him and yet it wasn't going to be that simple.

If she hadn't fallen asleep the way she had last night, Scarlett would already have started to assess that fact.

She had to assess it now, and yet how did she do that with any kind of clarity when all she could acknowledge was how much she still loved him?

Oh, Scarlett. You've placed yourself in an even more potentially hurtful state of heart and mind than the one you faced five years ago. Did he tell you that he's in love with you still? Did he tell you that anything about his situation has changed or will change?

Last night Scarlett hadn't wanted to think about it, but Lorenzo's attitude to his marriage...

'There has to be more of a reason for why you haven't divorced her.' Scarlett uttered the words and her business brain did click into place for a moment to let her see that this had to be so. Nothing else made sense.

'What do you mean?' He uttered the words in a tone that drew her gaze immediately to his face.

A tone that seemed defensive? *Yes.* Scarlett set her coffee cup down on the bedside table and looked him very directly in the eyes. 'Lorenzo–'

'I contacted the police before I woke you.' Lorenzo also set his coffee aside. 'All they could tell me was that they were still processing on the case. They will phone the moment they have anything they can tell us.'

His gaze roved over her hair and face before he seemed to recollect himself.

Scarlett drew a shaky breath and resisted the urge to tidy that hair, to raise her arms and try to check her appearance. 'I hope when you hear from the police again, they'll have something solid to tell you.' She hesitated. 'You didn't tell them that I was—?'

'Here? No.' His response was immediate, firm. 'And it's still very early. There's time for me to get you home before dawn breaks. I didn't bring up Marcella with them either. Not yet.'

So no one would know of their night together, because Scarlett had yet again given herself to a man who was not free to be given to. Just as she had given herself to this same man five years ago. And he was still avoiding the issue of his wife. Not by not discussing her with the police. But by not discussing her with Scarlett.

So where did that leave Scarlett?

It left her reaching inside herself for strength.

'I won't have an ongoing affair with you a second time.' The words cost her. The thought of never being in his arms again cost her more than Scarlett could have thought imaginable. But she had pushed them out. They were said. She needed to be respected, to have her needs respected. 'There's a gap in the things you told me last night. I'm guessing you didn't want to have to tell me the things that you did—'

'Does any man want to admit that he's been manipulated? That his career and life have suffered because of the vindictiveness of a woman he married as a childhood sweetheart and found out he didn't know at all?' The words burst out, seemed to shock him as they echoed in the quiet of the room.

Scarlett understood pride. Oh, she understood that. Her family was full of it. She'd wrapped it around herself when she went back to Australia after their affair.

For a time pride had been the only thing that enabled her to lift her head and stick out her chin and face down the world until after a while she started to be able to do it by herself once again.

'You *are* a proud man.' This, she knew, and even understood. 'You're also a strong one, and that is why I don't understand why you haven't divorced your wife in all this time. I don't see why, for example, you would let family expectations keep you locked into a situation that is clearly causing you harm and making you miserable. It doesn't make sense. Even Dante took the chance to get away from his bad situation the moment he saw a way out. And he's happier. He's no longer trying to make up excuses for his bruises.'

Lorenzo made an odd sound and turned his gaze away from her.

Scarlett froze.

Time seemed to freeze.

Things dropped together in Scarlett's mind like pieces of a puzzle. One that Scarlett hadn't known was there, and that... made her feel ill.

Lorenzo had made excuses for having a scratch on his face one time, a bruise on his chest another. For lots of scratches and bruises. He'd said they happened from taking spills off his motorcycle and yet he was a confident rider and he'd seemed to be that back then too, and he wasn't at all clumsy in any way that Scarlett had ever observed. The man worked with kitchen knives and never cut himself, and performed intricate tasks in the kitchen and always produced flawless results.

Dante had stolen and Lorenzo had talked to him, and had looked so sick when he realised Dante was being physically abused. Lorenzo had easily comprehended that whole situation. He'd so quickly agreed that bike riding could result in such accidents.

Oh, my God. Could it be? Could one horrid woman who would go so far as to cost him job after job even years after he had walked away from her... 'Was Marcella physically abusing you in your married life?' Scarlett whispered the words in an appalled, disbelieving tone.

He stood and stalked away from the bed in one angry movement. Then stopped. Shook his head. 'You were never to know this. No one was ever to know it.'

His words were low and filled with...shame.

Scarlett got out of the bed and took a step towards him.

His words stopped her. 'Do you think I want the world to know that my wife...abused me? I could never hold my head up. I never planned to let you know. I'd hoped if I explained the rest, that would satisfy you.'

He swung about and all his defensiveness *was* nothing but a front for a shame so deep.

'Oh, Lorenzo.' Tears pricked the backs of Scarlett's eyes. She forced them back. She couldn't let him see them. He might misunderstand her empathy and think it was pity.

'She was volatile. From the day we married she began to be verbally aggressive, to blame me for all sorts of things.' Once he started, he seemed determined to spit the words all out. Maybe they needed to get out. 'Nothing I did kept her happy. Because of her volatility I had doubts about trying for a baby but I thought it might be what she needed, a chance to bring out her maternal instincts, to soften her with that kind of love for her child.'

'But she couldn't conceive.' How long had Lorenzo dealt with this? Scarlett was so shocked, she could barely think!

'And as she faced that disappointment her aggression climbed until it reached the point of...'

He couldn't seem to make himself say it.

'Of attacking you?'

'I never retaliated, Scarlett.' His gaze was strong and truthful as he finally sought hers once more. 'I promise you, I never ever—'

'Of course you wouldn't have.' Her words were soft, accepting, equally truthful. Scarlett shook her head even as her heart ached to the depths for him. 'I know you, 'Renz. Of course you wouldn't have retaliated.'

His shoulders seemed to relax slightly as he absorbed her words. 'I tried to avoid arguments. I asked her to go to counselling. This wasn't something that I could take to family, or discuss with friends. I couldn't get her to seek help. Things got so bad that all I wanted was to get away from her. We'd been sleeping in separate rooms for months when I met you. I fell for you before I knew what had happened to me. I knew I needed to tell you, but I couldn't.'

He blew out a breath. 'I was afraid I'd lose you. It was hard to think straight. Finally I went to her and told her I loved you and asked her to release me. She threatened harm to you as well. I couldn't let that happen to you. In the end I lost you, but I knew you were safe at least and then...I left her, but she continued to hold power over me by impacting on my job future, by getting at me financially.

'I found her behaviour so disgusting that I couldn't go anywhere near her. The thought of trying to fight through for a divorce...' He paused and finally went on. 'What was the point? I no longer wanted to remarry so I left it.'

'She must have hurt you so much.' Scarlett didn't mean the strength of the physical attacks, and he seemed to understand this.

'If you told her she either has to agree to a divorce or you'll go to the police, tell them everything—'

'I could *lose* everything.' He glanced around him. 'I've worked hard to get back on my feet. I've been saving to try to start my own restaurant somewhere one day.'

When Scarlett came back to Monta Correnti, there'd been the problem of getting Luca's restaurant into a better place financially. Scarlett was working on that, and during their weekend cook-off she'd had a rather unorthodox idea about that. She thought it might work. In fact, Sorella offering to help out while the fire damage was fixed was almost like a sign. That situation just might be fixable. If Scarlett handled it with enough care.

But she did not know how Lorenzo's situation could be fixable. He wouldn't want to risk exposing what had happened to him, and yet his wife's behaviour had been so wrong.

Scarlett didn't know how to help him overcome any of this.

And while she searched her heart for answers, Lorenzo's face closed down and he seemed to draw deep into himself. 'I never wanted you to know this, Scarlett. It is a badge of shame that digs deep into my soul. Last night, what we shared. That shouldn't have happened. There's nowhere that we can go from here. Not…together. I shouldn't have taken that night with you.'

Even as his words cut through the secret hopes that Scarlett hadn't even realised had built themselves up so strongly within her, Lorenzo went on.

'No matter how we felt last night, now matter how much either of us needed…' He seemed to struggle to know how to go on. 'Five years ago I ignored the facts of my life and reached out for you. I learned then that I can't give you the things that you deserve, that I would want to give you. That…'

It hadn't changed.

That was what Lorenzo was about to say.

And Scarlett dug down inside *herself.* If she didn't take control of this conversation, and do it right now before this went any further, she didn't know if she would be able to keep herself pulled together.

Everything inside her hurt. She felt as though she'd been offered something so amazing, had been offered a second chance only to have it snatched back out of her hands. 'I came to Monta Correnti with certain goals in mind.'

Those goals hadn't included falling for Lorenzo a second time. That had happened, she couldn't undo that now, but she could get over it, just as she had done the first time. And she would. Scarlett felt numb inside, but she told herself she could do this. She could! He was rejecting her, and she *could* cope with this second rejection and not let it utterly crush her.

She patently ignored the fact that she hadn't seemed to do much of a job of getting over him the first time!

'My goals—' Were clearer now. 'My goals revolve around the way I relate to my family, and making a success of my work. Once I've achieved those goals I'll return to Australia and pick up my life there. Yes, that's what I'm going to do.'

That, and only that. She wouldn't remain here, torturing herself over him. 'I've got an idea that I think is what the restaurant needs. If I can get the relevant parties to agree on it, it should really ensure the financial security of Rosa for now and for the future. I'll have achieved that goal, and I'm going to achieve my family goals, too, so I can go back knowing that I've done the things I came here needing to do. I won't be here much longer.'

She would leave. That was all Scarlett could think. She would go back to Australia and not have to deal with these feelings. First she had to get through this day of realising she still loved him with all her heart, and knowing deep down that he did not love her in the same way.

Because if he did, he would find a way. Or ask her to help him find a way. Scarlett had a really good brain. She could help him figure out strategies to outsmart his wife and get himself fully free of Marcella. There had to be a way. But Lorenzo wasn't asking for that.

All he was saying was that they couldn't be together again in the way they had been last night. So it was hopeless, wasn't it? Hopeless and she was better off to cut her losses and walk away as quickly as she could.

Scarlett would start cutting those losses as of right now. She headed for Lorenzo's living room and the carry bag she hadn't touched since her arrival. 'I need five minutes to shower but after that I'd like you to take me back to my bedsit. If I don't feel safe later I'll stay with my mother or another family member, but this…'

She shook her head. She couldn't think. All she could do was feel far too much hurt, and so much more, threatening to consume her because in the end he couldn't give himself to her.

What did that leave except a great well of nothing?

Lorenzo's telephone rang.

Scarlett left him to answer it, and closed herself into the bathroom.

Whatever came, whatever happened next, she had to bear it, be a professional. Most of all she had to bear the knowledge that he cared, but he didn't love her the way she loved him. He didn't, or he would work with her to figure this out. She wanted to help him get past his feelings of shame.

She'd told him it wasn't his fault, and that he had acted honourably. She understood a man wouldn't be able to accept that easily. She wished she could help him find that acceptance.

Scarlett had her limits, too. She couldn't let herself be crushed and broken by a love that he couldn't give back to her in the same measure. She'd struggled to survive the last time. She didn't know if she could survive a second time.

It was time for Scarlett to get herself organised, get Rosa fully and finally organised and sort out her issues with her family, and…leave Italy.

Before her love for Lorenzo destroyed her.

CHAPTER TWELVE

'I WONDER if Scarlett realises what she's achieved by getting Lisa even to the point of being prepared to consider this idea,' Romano said to Lorenzo as they stood outside Lorenzo's home.

It was Wednesday morning. Lorenzo had been leaving Lisa's when Romano had dropped Jackie and Scarlett there, before taking Lorenzo home. The last two days had been busy with police reports. The restaurant, despite or perhaps in part also because of the arson attempt, was doing great business, and working in co-operation with Sorella's to ensure they could seat everyone and get on with things.

Scarlett was forging ahead with family and work. Romano had boasted just now about his beautiful daughter, Kate, and said that Scarlett had spent hours poring over Kate's photos with her sister Jackie.

Scarlett seemed to be finding forgiveness for herself for her part in Jackie losing her child for so long. Soon Scarlett would have resolved all her issues with family, and, with her work done at Rosa, Scarlett would leave.

So why let that happen when you're deep in love with her and don't want to lose her? Why let your pride—?

'The indoor dining will be back in business tomorrow, so I hear?' Romano took the newspaper Lorenzo handed to him that featured an article about the fire at Rosa.

'Uh, yes. Yes, it will.' Lorenzo couldn't concentrate, because he'd fought these thoughts for two days, fought them since he and Scarlett made love.

He'd fought for the sake of…his pride and because he felt such shame that he had somehow ended up being abused by Marcella. And maybe he never could have Scarlett and maybe he never would be good enough for her, but didn't he owe it to her to at least let her know that he loved her? That he had never stopped loving her? Couldn't there maybe, somehow, be a way for them?

If Lorenzo could figure out how to ensure Scarlett couldn't be hurt by it, couldn't he finally break the ties with Marcella and be free? And if Scarlett *was* prepared to give him even a chance to love her, maybe they could go back to Australia together and start over there where Marcella, even if she wanted to, couldn't cause them problems?

Or they could stay right here and…face it out together? 'I can tell Scarlett. I'm at least going to tell her!'

Romano raised his brows but, perhaps wisely, said nothing.

And as though Lorenzo's thoughts had conjured her, a car drew to a stop on the street outside his home and Scarlett stepped out.

Romano murmured some words that Lorenzo didn't really listen to, something about it looking like Scarlett had borrowed one of her mother's cars. He nodded to Lorenzo and left.

Lorenzo only had eyes for Scarlett. Love welled inside him and it took a moment for him to realise that Scarlett appeared…upset?

'Did you say yes?' She walked right up until they stood just a hand's reach away from each other. 'Did you say yes when my mother offered you a better-paid position working alongside her other chef in the Sorella kitchen?'

'Did Lisa tell you she made that offer?' He was surprised. He'd got the impression that Lisa had thrown out the hint about that more as if she felt she wouldn't be doing her business-related duty if she didn't than anything.

She'd invited him to the villa, told him he was a great chef and Sorella would benefit by having him on board as a second chef in their kitchens, and then she had waited.

So, in point of fact, she hadn't exactly *offered*. 'Your mother threw out a hint. I told her how happy I am at Rosa and how good Luca's been to me. If anything, Scarlett, I came away with the impression that I'd passed some kind of test by not trying to pick up on her hint about changing jobs.'

'Because you have no right to just turn around—' Scarlett broke off. For a moment her mouth worked and no sound came out. And then her gaze narrowed and she drew a deep breath. 'So you're not leaving Rosa to work at Sorella?'

'No.' He lifted his hands, palms up.

'Maybe Mamma really is considering *my* suggestion to her, then.' Some of the heat seemed to leave Scarlett and she cast one deep, torn glance at him before she dropped her gaze.

'Your idea to combine the two restaurants so both of them can function with greater success and stronger profit margins?' When she seemed shocked, he held up a hand. 'Romano mentioned it just now. I understand this is something that needs to be kept under wraps while you all work on Lisa, and that you're not telling Luca about it yet so you don't raise any false hopes in him.'

Scarlett slowly nodded. 'And so we can figure out how to put it to him without him having an implosion.' She drew a breath. 'My sisters are both behind the idea. Jackie and I have talked with Elizabeth about it by phone conference. Isabella supports the idea, too.'

'And Lisa?' If Scarlett had come storming here to accuse him of letting himself be headhunted by her mother—

'Didn't know why I excused myself as abruptly as I did.' Scarlett sighed. 'I don't want to be at loggerheads with anyone in my family. I…love Mamma. I see myself in her and her in me, and I'd like to think we could be a bit closer as mother and daughter. I. need to be closer to the Italian side of my family. I need to let them all in, to stop shutting them out and shutting myself away. Jackie and I talked about that. And then she took me to meet Kate yesterday. That…really…'

She couldn't seem to go on and she turned her head away, but Lorenzo saw her throat work and he decided they'd had quite enough of standing around outside. 'Come into the house, Scarlett.'

He didn't wait for her to agree or give permission. Rather, he gently clasped her hand in his and took one step, and when she looked up and into his eyes he took another, and led her into the house and sat side by side with her on the sofa. 'What happened when you met Jackie's daughter?'

'My sister shone all over with happiness, and Kate is a sweet girl. Kate's other mother was there and…it was all fine.' Emotion brought a bright sheen of moisture to her eyes. 'Jackie is so happy now. Her happiness *is* allowing her to let go of past hurts. I thought she might never really be able to forgive me but, instead, she only wants to share her happiness with me. The two of us came away from that meeting with Kate closer than we've ever been.'

'That's a good thing, Scarlett.' He drew a breath and gently stroked his thumb over the back of her hand.

And Scarlett seemed to realise where she was and what she was doing. She drew her hand away and looked at him. 'I came here on a burst of anger. I thought you'd walked away from your responsibilities at Rosa, or that you were going to.'

'You don't want anything to go wrong there. You're working to put the restaurant in a great place. I have no desire to abandon ship there. One day I hope to have my own restaurant, but that will be many years from now. Though…I would leave to…forge a new start with—'

But he was getting ahead of himself. Way, way ahead. He searched her face and wished that he could see more of what was inside her. Maybe that would come. All he knew for now was that he had this opportunity and he didn't want to lose it. 'I'm glad you came here, Scarlett. I'd decided that I needed to seek you out. I don't want to let you leave, go back to Australia, without telling you…'

Scarlett looked into Lorenzo's eyes and told herself she shouldn't have come looking for him. She could as easily have brought this up with him at Rosa, during working hours.

Had she seized on any excuse to have contact with him? She'd tried so hard to keep her distance emotionally, even as they had worked side by side for the past two days in the aftermath of the arson attempt on Rosa. 'What did you want to discuss? The arson? The clean-up? Rosa's indoor dining should be back to normal and useable tomorrow.'

She was dodging. She knew it, but she wasn't sure if she could take anything more.

'And the police are dealing with the kitchen hand and his girlfriend.' Lorenzo straightened his shoulders. 'It's good that they've admitted to the crime, and I'm pleased to know that Marcella didn't do it.'

'But she *could* do such a thing. You can't predict how low your…wife will stoop to continue to make your life miserable.'

'That's in a way, what I want, and need, to say to you.' Lorenzo said the words in a low tone.

Scarlett searched his face. 'I don't really understand. What else is there to say?'

'I don't want to lose you a second time, Scarlett.' The words burst out of Lorenzo and he drew a deep breath.

Scarlett's heart started to thump in her chest. She wanted to leap up from the couch and run and keep on running. But she also wanted to stay right here and hope for things that she couldn't afford to hope for.

Before she could do anything, Lorenzo went on. 'For the past two days as you've gone about your work, making sure Rosa continued on, working to convince key family members to embrace the idea of combining the two restaurants, I've watched you moving towards leaving and…'

He shook his head. 'You're amazing. You've come up with a plan that would benefit both Sorella and Rosa, if it can be implemented. I doubt there'd be many things that you couldn't make happen, if you set your mind to them. You're a strong woman, Scarlett. Strong *and* gentle *and* giving to your family. You've done all of this…for them.'

'In a way I guess I have, but I did it for me as well.' She'd wanted to find ways to draw closer, to feel a part of them.

They were still a volatile and diverse bunch of people, but Scarlett did feel closer. 'The fire, even though it was a rotten thing to happen, drew us all together too.'

'It drew *us* together that night, as well. You and me.' Lorenzo turned to face her, and when he reached for her hand again he looked so serious as he searched for words. 'I told you of the shame of Marcella's treatment of me. And of her threats. I couldn't see a way to get fully free of her, without her causing further harm to my career, or without the truth of her behaviour coming out and…my pride didn't want to deal with people knowing.'

'She's the one who should feel shame!' The words burst out of Scarlett. She couldn't hold them back. 'There's never an acceptable reason for physical violence in that kind of situation. *You* were strong, Lorenzo. You showed your strength and your character by refusing to retaliate and by trying to get help for her.'

'I've thought about that since we discussed it.' He cleared his throat. 'Thank you for your faith in me. It means more than you probably realise.'

His eyes looked into hers with such...love?

Scarlett's breath caught in her throat. ''Renz?'

'I still love you, Scarlett.' His words switched to Italian. Scarlett guessed he didn't even notice that he'd done it as he went on. 'Even more than I did five years ago. I never stopped loving you. It stayed inside me. I think it would have for ever. I love you with everything. I don't expect you to feel the same but I need you to know that you have my heart. It's yours. It always will be.'

What did he mean? Were these just words again? Words that would go into *her* heart, but wouldn't change anything? Scarlett choked back a sob and *her* words burst out. 'I love you, too, but I can't walk that path a second time. I can't give myself into your hands again and only get crumbs in return.'

'Will you give me one day?' He asked the question in earnestness. 'Please, Scarlett? One day to get my life in order and come to you with my heart in my hands? Just say you'll give me that chance?'

Two parts of Scarlett heard his words. Heart and head. Her head said take care of herself, don't run the risk, don't hope, don't trust.

But her heart...

'I'll give you your day.' She stood from the sofa on shaky legs and forced herself to walk to the door. 'You'll need to ask Isabella to cover for you at work while you take care of what you need to take care of.' She wanted to help him, but she understood that this was something he was going to need to do by himself.

Lorenzo nodded. 'I'll speak to her.'

Scarlett left the house.

And Lorenzo…set out to take back his life. His life, and his freedom.

And his future.

CHAPTER THIRTEEN

'THIS is lovely.' Scarlett uttered the words around a stampede of butterflies that were doing hob-nailed cartwheels in her tummy. They seemed to be fluttering around in her throat, too.

It was the following day, late lunch time. She and Lorenzo were sitting on a blanket at the same quiet mountain knoll they'd visited in the middle of the night.

Isabella was covering for Lorenzo back at Rosa. The Sorella chef was helping.

Scarlett wasn't sure if she should be pleased about that co-operative effort, or embarrassed, because apparently the chef seemed to think he was helping the course of love for Lorenzo and Scarlett. The man apparently had a soft romantic streak.

'This has been a long time coming and I wanted to do it right,' Lorenzo said as he uncorked a bottle of wine and poured some into two glasses. He placed one glass in he hand.

His fingers shook slightly, and somehow that small sign of uncertainty helped Scarlett to relax a little. He took the lid from a wicker picnic basket and drew out fresh strawberries and tiny heart-shaped chocolate tarts in a crystal basket. Tied to the handle of the basket was a cream hair ribbon that matched pearl earrings and a drop necklace. A ribbon that Lorenzo had tucked into his pocket against his heart…

'When did you get time—?'

'I haven't slept.' His fingers caressed that ribbon with gentle reverence. 'How could I when I was waiting for this? And…I wanted to spoil you.'

So he had cooked for her. He'd made beautiful chocolate desserts and teamed them with fresh fruit and a light red wine that tasted just right, and tied his gift together with her hair ribbon. Scarlett sipped. She couldn't eat just now. Her tummy was in too many knots! Instead she swallowed and tried to smile. 'Thank you.'

'Yesterday, I saw a lawyer. Then I warned my family that I intended to have the divorce I've wanted for years whether they can ever approve of it or not, and…I went to see Marcella.' His lips pressed together.

'Did you take your lawyer with you as a witness?' Scarlett set her wine down and gave him all her attention.

'No.' He shook his head. 'That confrontation with her was something that I had to do for myself, and…I did it. I chose a public place. When I told her I *would* divorce her she tried to…grab hold of my arm. But I just got up from the table and made it clear if she tried again I would consider it an assault and report it to the police as such.'

He drew a breath. 'It was a coffee shop in her village. People heard the altercation. Some of them may have seen the way she tried to dig her nails into my arm, and that I had to…remove her touch. Some may have heard me say I would bring the police into it.'

'That gossip could filter back to Monta Correnti.' Scarlett bit her lip.

His smile was a little forced, perhaps, but it was also determined. 'If it does, I will hold my head up. I've realised *I* know that I did no wrong and didn't deserve her treatment, and, that I tried to be understanding and help her.'

'In the end that's what really matters.' Scarlett was so glad that he'd realised this!

Scarlett wasn't sure how it had happened, but she realised that *her* hand had reached for Lorenzo's and she had clasped his fingers in hers. His hand wrapped around her fingers, too. She said quietly, 'What happened after that?'

'I laid out my terms. I told her I'd already had legal advice, that I would not tolerate her interfering in my life ever again, and made it clear that I would no longer try to hide from her behaviour past or present.' He shrugged and he made that shrug look as though that hadn't been difficult at all, and taking that action had been easy. 'I walked out while she was still gaping.'

Scarlett laughed.

Oh, not because it was funny but because… 'I'm so proud of you, Lorenzo.' And as quickly as she laughed, emotion clogged her throat. She blinked fiercely. 'I'm really, really proud of you.'

'I'll have my freedom, Scarlett. After this length of separation, my lawyer says there's no way she could fight it when I file for divorce.'

Scarlett's heart started to thunder all over again. 'That's— that's good.'

Sunshine dappled over them through the leafy shade of trees as he drew both her hands into his. 'I'm still struggling not to be ashamed of what happened with her. It's something that may continue to raise its head now and then for a long time, I think, but I'm prepared for Marcella to do her worst. If she pushes me, I *will* go to the police. Also if she tried to cause *you* any harm—'

'I would go to the police right along with you.' Scarlett

squeezed his hands. 'For your sake I hope it doesn't all come out and I hope she doesn't attempt to come anywhere near either of us. But if that happens, will you please try to remind yourself that you were the strong one? You refused to harm her or lower yourself to her level.'

He drew a shallow breath. 'I might not have a lot else to offer, but, Scarlett, if you would take it, I would offer you... my heart. I want to love and cherish you for the rest of my life, be at your side, wake up with you, fall asleep with you.' His gaze dropped to the chocolate tarts and in the midst of the emotion one corner of his mouth turned up. 'Cook for you. I am a chef. I will always be that, no matter what.'

And his voice deepened. 'I want to marry you. If there is any way you can find it in your heart to give me a second chance, I want to marry you and spend all the rest of my days loving you. I'm hoping, if you'll give me that chance, that love can grow within you for me again. That I maybe haven't completely ruined any chance of that with you.'

He drew a slow, deep breath. 'I've made some mistakes. The situation with Marcella seemed to get further and further out of control as time passed. I felt helpless to address it and I let pride and shame get in the way of seeing clearly. I didn't want to upset my family either, or hers, but in the end they're not the ones living my life. I am, and I want my chance to be truly happy. There's only one person I can ever have that with. She's sitting here with me right now.'

Lorenzo had humbled himself for her sake. He'd faced a situation that had taken him to the depths of shame, had been prepared to make all of that public if he had to, in order to buy his freedom to ask her for this.

Scarlett's heart melted. All of her melted in love and acceptance for him. And Scarlett knew that she, too, had to be completely truthful and open with him. 'I didn't handle myself well, either, when we separated. I didn't handle myself well for a long time, long before I even met you.'

She'd run, run all the way to Australia to her father and that side of the family, but Scarlett had never addressed what sent her out of Italy. 'I knew I'd done something bad to Jackie when I threw that letter away. As time passed and I grew up and realised the full extent of my actions I hid the guilt behind ignoring the family.'

'But if you were only a child—' Lorenzo wanted to forgive the issue. That fact was written all over him.

Scarlett loved him for that generosity, but if he wanted to be able to move on in his own life and to move on with her he needed to hear that no one was perfect and that *Scarlett* was far from perfect. 'The time came when I should have addressed that issue with Jackie. I dodged doing that. Even when I came back here this time and Jackie wanted me to look at photos of Kate, at first I didn't want to do it.'

'But you did, and now you've met your niece.' His fingers tightened over hers.

Scarlett drew a breath and felt the squeeze of Lorenzo's fingers, and squeezed back and smiled. 'It went really well. Jackie only wants to look forwards, I think, not behind her now. She says I need to do the same. I needed to feel resolved with my family, to let them back into my life. I didn't want to stay shut away from them, and them shut away from me.'

'I think your sister is wise.'

'A lot of people think I'm like Mamma, and that Mamma is very cold, but I don't think even Mum is really that frozen inside.' Scarlett drew a breath. 'She's done some things. Maybe we all have. But I've started to see the chinks in her armour, too.'

She leaned forward and said confidentially, 'Maybe it's a time for the women of my family to revisit first loves, because

I learned today that the man Mamma was with the night of the fire was Rafe Puccini.'

'Didn't he help launch your mother's modelling career years ago?'

Scarlett nodded her head. 'Yes, and he opened up his family palazzo for Lizzie's wedding. He and Mum were flirting then, but I didn't think anything would come of it.' Scarlett shrugged. 'And maybe it won't. I guess we'll have to wait and see, but…Mamma's voice changes when she speaks his name.'

'Would you mind if she found love with him?' Lorenzo stroked his fingers over the back of her hand.

Scarlett absorbed his touch, felt the love within it. Turned her hand and clasped his. 'No. I'd be happy for her. Love is worth being happy about.'

'It is.' He smiled, and Scarlett smiled, and they both fell silent.

Finally she said, 'My life has been far from perfect, too, Lorenzo. You don't have to ask me to grow to love you. I already do. Deep in my heart I don't think I ever stopped. I love you now more than ever before. So if *you* can accept me with all my history and my flaws and shortcomings, but knowing that I will give all of my heart to you and not hold anything back, I…want to try. *I want to marry you.*'

Relief and joy and happiness and love, all washed over his face and straight away she was in his arms, crushed close while he rained kisses into her hair and over her face and neck and finally their lips met and it felt as if it really was a promise for their future.

When they drew apart, Scarlett looked into rich brown eyes that she had grown to know and love so much. She saw no shadows whatsoever, just happiness. Her own happiness burst forth inside her then as she truly knew that they would indeed have their lives together, a happy future. 'If Marcella causes trouble I'll help you. Though the need will never arise with Luca. He said you're an honourable man and anyone could see that, and he was right!'

Maybe Scarlett had always known that, too, deep down inside. She'd just needed to work it out. And now she had.

She hesitated as she wondered about the logistics of their future. 'If it would be better for you, we *could* go to Australia and live there.'

In truth, Scarlett wasn't sure now if she wanted that or not. A part of her wanted to stay in Italy and another part did want to return to Australia. She loved both sides of her family, but most of them were here.

'I'm trying to get to know all this side of my family, but it's not a quick job.' She shook her head. 'I have cousins I haven't even met that are children of Luca's.'

'Don't stress too much about it, Scarlett.' Lorenzo's hands gently rubbed over her shoulders as he held her against his chest. 'It doesn't matter to me where I live. If Australia is better, we can live there. If here is best, I'm happy to stay. Now that I've finally confronted Marcella and insisted that she completely release me, I have a feeling that she'll be forced to realise she truly has no hold over me any more.'

'And *your* family?' Scarlett would stand by him through anything, and she smiled as she said, 'I've had some practice dealing with stubborn family members.' She hesitated and added sheepishly, 'And, I guess, *being* one.'

He laughed before his expression sobered. 'I've yet to decide whether to tell the truth to my parents. I'm not sure if they'd ever be able to understand. I'm going to tell my brothers, though. They're good men. I'm looking forward to you meeting them.'

Scarlett would cope with meeting his parents, too. 'I want you to meet my dad. You'll like him. He's a good guy.' She gave a teasing smile. 'Even if he does eat mass-produced Australian pizza now and then.'

'I'll enjoy meeting him.' Lorenzo brushed his knuckles over her cheek. 'I don't want to leave Rosa in the lurch, either, though I know I'm not irreplaceable.'

'You are to me.' And they would support each other through whatever came their way, whatever choices they needed to make and actions they needed to take. 'We'll sort it all out, 'Renz.'

Something told Scarlett that this big, boisterous family that had been through so many ups and downs would also support them when they found out that she and Lorenzo were in love, and planning to get married.

She wrapped her arms around Lorenzo's middle. 'We're going to be part of a big family.' Scarlett would need to get to know Lorenzo's family, too, and that might not be easy at first but they would get there.

He squeezed back, loving her with his touch and his gaze and his heart. His expression sobered. 'And we will be our own family, too, and maybe one day...'

'Have children of our own.' Scarlett swallowed as she thought of it. Bearing Lorenzo's child. 'I would like that. When we're both ready.'

'Until I get you a ring, will you wear this as a sign of my love?' Lorenzo removed the medallion from around his neck and gently closed the chain behind her neck. The gold disc settled between her breasts. It was still warm from his body. 'I don't think I ever told you, but the medallion was a gift from my late grandmother. I loved her, and...it would please me for you to wear it.'

Scarlett swallowed hard and her fingers rose to touch the chain. 'I will wear it with all of *my* love.'

'Thank you, Scarlett. Thank you for the gift of *you* in my life.' Lorenzo laid her gently in the soft grass, and they rested in the dappled shade of the tree and gave themselves time. To whisper and talk and kiss and think about the future.

To eat chocolate tarts and strawberries and sip a little more wine.

And to dream and know that, this time, their dreams were *going* to come true!

HARLEQUIN Romance.

Coming Next Month

Available October 12, 2010

LARGER-PRINT BOOKS!
GET 2 FREE LARGER-PRINT NOVELS PLUS
2 FREE GIFTS!

From the Heart, For the Heart

HRLP10R2

HARLEQUIN®

A Romance

FOR EVERY MOOD™

Spotlight on

Inspirational

Wholesome romances
that touch the heart and soul.

See the next page
to enjoy a sneak peek from
the Love Inspired® inspirational series.

*See below for a sneak peek at
our inspirational line, Love Inspired®.
Introducing HIS HOLIDAY BRIDE
by bestselling author Jillian Hart*

Autumn Granger gave her horse rein to slide toward the town's new sheriff.

"Hey, there." The man in a brand-new Stetson, black T-shirt, jeans and riding boots held up a hand in greeting. He stepped away from his four-wheel drive with "Sheriff" in black on the doors and waded through the grasses. "I'm new around here."

"I'm Autumn Granger."

"Nice to meet you, Miss Granger. I'm Ford Sherman, from Chicago." He knuckled back his hat, revealing the most handsome face she'd ever seen. Big blue eyes contrasted with his sun-tanned complexion.

"I'm guessing you haven't seen much open land. Out here, you've got to keep an eye on cows or they're going to tear your vehicle apart."

"What?" He whipped around. Sure enough, mammoth black-and-white creatures had started to gnaw on his four-wheel drive. They clustered like a mob, mouths and tongues and teeth bent on destruction. One cow tried to pry the wiper off the windshield, another chewed on the side mirror. Several leaned through the open window, licking the seats.

"Move along, little dogie." He didn't know the first thing about cattle.

The entire herd swiveled their heads to study him curiously. Not a single hoof shifted. The animals soon returned to chewing, licking, digging through his possessions.

Autumn laughed, a warm and wonderful sound. "Thanks,

I needed that." She then pulled a bag from behind her saddle and waved it at the cows. "Look what I have, guys. Cookies."

Cows swung in her direction, and dozens of liquid brown eyes brightened with cookie hopes. As she circled the car, the cattle bounded after her. The earth shook with the force of their powerful hooves.

"Next time, you're on your own, city boy." She tipped her hat. The cowgirl stayed on his mind, the sweetest thing he had ever seen.

Will Ford be able to stick it out in the country
to find out more about Autumn?
Find out in HIS HOLIDAY BRIDE
by bestselling author Jillian Hart,
available in October 2010
only from Love Inspired®.

FROM #1 *NEW YORK TIMES*
AND *USA TODAY* BESTSELLING AUTHOR

DEBBIE MACOMBER

Mrs. Miracle on 34th Street...

This Christmas, Emily Merkle (just call her Mrs. Miracle)
is working in the toy department at Finley's, the last
family-owned department store in Manhattan.

Her boss (who happens to be the owner's son) has placed
an order for a large number of high-priced robots, which
he hopes will give the business a much-needed boost. In
fact, Jake Finley's counting on it.

Holly Larson is counting on that robot, too. She's been
looking after her eight-year-old nephew, Gabe, ever since
her widowed brother was deployed overseas. Holly plans
to buy Gabe a robot—which she can't afford—because
she's determined to make Christmas special.

But this Christmas will be different—thanks to Mrs.
Miracle. Next to bringing children joy, her favorite activity
is giving romance a nudge. Fortunately, Jake and Holly
are receptive to her "hints." And thanks to Mrs. Miracle,
Christmas takes on new meaning for Jake. For all of them!

Call Me Mrs. Miracle

**Available wherever books are sold
September 28!**